THE WAY HOME

"That is the way of the Maelstrom," the greenish-gray Kalira named Harxae said. "After you have been here as long as we, you will understand."

"Right," David said. "How long have you been here?"

Harxae and Gavwin stared at one another for a moment, telepathically communicating, then Gavwin said, "We have been here for two hundred and seventy-three of your years. We are relative newcomers. The Shard have been here for thousands."

"Have you—I mean, can you—"

"There is no escape," Harxae said.

David leaned forward and looked out the window, where the white cloud surrounding the probe still swirled softly. "Are you sure? Look at that cable. The other end is on the other side. If I followed it, wouldn't I end up back home?"

Both aliens were silent for a few seconds, before Harxae said, "We don't know. Nobody has ever managed to leave a lifeline before . . ."

VOR: THE MAELSTROM

Vor: Into the Maelstrom
by Loren L. Coleman

Vor: The Playback War
by Lisa Smedman

Vor: Island of Power
by Dean Wesley Smith

Available from Warner Aspect®

THE RESCUE

DON ELLIS

ASPECT®

WARNER BOOKS

A Time Warner Company

WARNER BOOKS EDITION

Cover design by Don Puckey
Cover illustration by Donato
Cover logo design by Jim Nelson

Warner Books, Inc.
1271 Avenue of the Americas
New York, NY 10020

Visit our Web site at
www.twbookmark.com

W A Time Warner Company

Printed in the United States of America

First Printing: July 2000

10 9 8 7 6 5 4 3 2 1

THE RESCUE

1

David Hutchins had just gotten to the trickiest part of repairing the base's nuclear generator—aligning the fuel injector and the ignition lasers to meet in the exact center of the reaction chamber—when the communicator at his hip vibrated. He didn't want to answer, but the Union situation here on Mars was too tenuous for him to ignore any calls.

Leaving the lasers hot, he slipped the commlink off his belt and thumbed it on. "Hutchins," he said absently, his mind still on the generator problem.

"David, this is Raedawn. I need you down here right away. Something is happening to Earth." She sounded either excited or upset, and that caught David's attention. Captain Raedawn Corona, the expedition's intelligence officer, was known for her trademark cool.

"You mean something is happening *on* Earth." Even as he spoke, David leaned over and peered into the exposed reaction chamber. The lasers crossed in a perfect six-sided star as they poured their energy into one central point. A little squirt of deuterium to that same point would flash to plasma in an instant, and the magnetic containment field would keep that plasma squeezed into a tiny, ultra-hot mass until it underwent fusion.

"David, you're not listening. Something is happening *to* Earth. And to Luna as well."

"Okay, okay, calm down. I hear you. Something is happening *to* Earth. Like what? What kind of something?" The generator problem still tugged at his mind. The containment field had already been tested. All he had to do was align the fuel injector and the generator would be ready to return to service.

"If I knew that, do you think I'd be calling you?" Raedawn's voice rose in pitch. "The reports are garbled. A . . . a thing has appeared in space. It's like a monster dark cloud with arms reaching out toward Earth creating havoc everywhere they touch."

David straightened up again as he listened. The generator problem would just have to wait.

"It's been going on for the last few minutes," she said. He could tell from her voice she was scared—another first. "Ten at most. Plus light-lag, of course."

He calculated mentally. Mars was about seven light-minutes from Earth at the moment. If something was going on out there, it had been happening for about a quarter of an hour.

"David, are you there? David?"

He reached out to the generator control panel and switched off the lasers. "I'm on my—"

"Get down here," Raedawn snapped. "Now! I need your analysis." She disconnected abruptly.

"Is that so?" David muttered, deactivating the communicator and hooking it back onto his belt. Heading toward the door, he stumbled over some scrap metal pieces he'd left lying on the floor, and he cursed under his breath. They'd only been on Mars two days and already his lab was a maze of dismantled equipment, scattered tools, and sundry other items.

But the mess had a purpose. David was the expedition's chief science officer, with a specialty in physics. He was also a master of improvisation who could turn his expertise to the most ingenious practical applications. That was one of the reasons he'd been assigned to the Mars mission. He could make a telescope out of a couple of empty beer flasks and a liter of clear water or devise an air scrubber from a cooling fan and a dead carbonyl battery.

Exiting the lab, he hurried down the ragged rock corridor leading to the cavern housing the communications center. The entire base was underground, concealing it from the Neo-Sovs as well as from the harsh Martian environment. It was a warren of ancient lava tubes in the Noctis Labyrinthis region near the three major Tharsis volcanoes. They hadn't even needed to tunnel. A tech crew had sealed the cracks in the ancient caverns and pressurized them with oxygen, and the Union forces had moved right in. In most places the last of the lava had even pooled to make flat, hard floors.

David's lab was a long walk from the command center, but not as long as the same distance would have been on Earth. Mars's two-fifths gravity let him take loping strides that sped him along fast enough to feel the wind on his face. He managed to dodge the masses of cable snaking across the floor and hanging from the tunnel walls, but accidentally clipped his head on one of the hastily strung lights that lined the tunnel.

The base represented a major accomplishment for the Union. Until now, the Neo-Sovs had wiped out, to a man, every previous Union attempt to challenge their stranglehold on Mars. This time, however, the Union had succeeded.

Upon landing, the expedition had immediately broken into smaller groups, maintaining cover by laying booby traps and false trails to throw off the Neo-Sovs. The plan was to establish a secret command base while smaller units conducted guerrilla operations from satellite camps. The Neo-Soviet empire was bent on dominating all of humanity, and the North American Union was equally determined to stop it.

Colonel Kuranda, the expedition commander, had sent their three ships to an open-ended cavern several kilometers to the north. From there the craft could come and go without detection if the pilots took them out on agravs until they were well away. Those ships had started life as supply shuttles, but once unloaded on Mars, they'd been converted immediately into reconnaissance scouts and troop transports.

A platoon of Union soldiers made up the military core of the expedition, but not everybody was a grunt. David was a captain in Space Command, and the team also included a physician, additional medical personnel, and maybe half a dozen other specialists. Including Raedawn Corona, their intel officer. She was good at her job, if a bit prickly.

David picked his way over the last in a series of small generators and followed the lava tube's gentle curve toward the left, which took him to the entrance of the comm center. He stepped inside.

"Okay, Raedawn, here I am. What've you got so far?"

"What do you want?" she asked. "Diameter? Density? Spectral signature?"

"That'll do for a start."

"Too bad. It doesn't have any of that. Come and see for yourself. It's got these arms like tentacles reaching out in all directions from a central blotch of fuzzy gray stuff that doesn't actually emit or reflect light. It's just attenuating the starlight from behind it, and I don't see any absorption lines, either. It's more like a hole in space than an actual cloud."

David stepped up to the monitors as she spoke. Seeing the monstrous size of the cloud, he felt the first real jolt of alarm since Raedawn's call. The thing stretched from Earth to Lunar orbit, not even including the multiple arms. "What are the chances those arms could reach all the way to Mars?"

Raedawn's laugh was a quick, precise tool, a vehicle for expressing contempt, derision, and occasionally even humor. Until now he'd never heard it express bafflement. "Ha! Who knows? Ten minutes ago I would've sworn something like this couldn't even exist."

She sat in a swivel chair at the controls of the command panel. Around her were racks of transceivers and decoders optically linked to the phone, vid, and radio switchboards.

David noticed the way her short, dark hair stuck straight up on the left side, probably from being pulled in her nervous agitation. He also noted the black jacket hanging from one side of her chair, another first. In the short time he'd known Raedawn, he'd never seen her without that jacket on, even in the hottest of temperatures. But her bare arms glistened with sweat now, and the front of her black T-shirt was damp in spots, too.

He shook his head slightly and focused on the screens. "Let's see what's going on," he said, looking over her shoulder.

Raedawn had propped up five flat panel monitors in front of her, and more lay on the desktop. She shuffled through those until she found one that showed a city on fire, with a dark streak flickering back and forth across the sky overhead.

"That's the live hovercam feed from Denver," she said. "Live at the time, anyway. It's time-lagged about ten min-

utes instead of seven because I had to oversample the signal
and reprocess it to account for all the interference. Whatever
that thing is, it messes with the feed something fierce." The
transmissions were coming from Earth, beamed directly to
the stealth satellite the Union had orbiting Mars. It was set
up to show routine scans of the planet, in addition to providing a way to send and receive direct communications.

The scene on the monitor was still shot through with
static despite the signal processing. It showed traffic hopelessly snarled while crowds of people ran in all directions in
the streets below. Cars left the pattern as drivers attempted
manual control. Two of them collided and tumbled to the
ground from twenty or thirty stories up, taking another five
or six cars with them on their way down.

"Looks like total chaos," he murmured. "How much of
the planet is like this?"

Raedawn handed him the stack of screens. There were
easily a dozen of them, each one only a couple millimeters
thick and all of them showing similar scenes of destruction.
Denver was the largest city in actual flames, but one screen
showed a huge gash torn into Earth, with hot magma welling
up inside it. Seawater pouring into the submerged end
flashed to steam where it hit the magma, billowing up in
huge clouds that hid the ocean as winds carried them east-
ward.

"That's the 'scope feed," she said, referring to the
stealthed telescope the Union expedition had planted on
Deimos, one of the Mars moons, before landing. The telescope was directed at the Earth-Moon system, and the image
was clear as a photo.

"My God." David squinted at the gash looking for any
sign of life left on the ground, but the scale was too large. The
gash had to be twenty or thirty kilometers long, and at least

two or three kilometers wide. Not even a fusion bomb could do that. Unlike the image of Denver aflame, he couldn't really comprehend the magnitude of it.

"No reports or other communications?" he asked.

Raedawn shook her head. "I suspect they've got better things to do than feed us updates. Besides, the interference is getting so bad I doubt a single message would make it through. We're only getting this much because I can compare redundant feeds off multiple satellites."

He looked at the displays again. There was plenty of information there, none of it good. "Are you recording all this?"

"I have a brain."

"Surprise, surprise." He checked the access number for the top screen in his hand, then reached over her shoulder and pressed the hot key on her main screen that turned his into an auxiliary control panel. He took a half-dozen more screens with him to a desk behind her, velcroed them together in an upright arc in front of him, and started tapping in commands.

There was no point sifting through scrambled signals for what he wanted. Within seconds he had a spectral analysis, gravimetric readings, radiation levels, and a dozen other parameters on display. None of the data made any sense, but he sifted through it looking for patterns, connections, anything that might shed some light on what was going on. After a few minutes he switched to optical and just watched with his own two eyes.

Earth looked like a bright blue-and-white butterfly that had been caught in a spiderweb. A high-voltage spiderweb, crackling with lightning bolts that spanned continents and inhabited by a spider with hundreds of twitching black legs that raced back and forth across its surface. Part of him wanted to jump up and down and scream and yank his hair out, but another part was mesmerized by the interplay of unknown forces. He clung desperately to that part, knowing any help he could offer the beleaguered planet would come from rational thought, not emotional reaction.

"Where the hell is the energy coming from to power that thing?" he murmured to himself.

Raedawn turned half around in her chair. "What was that?"

"Just talking to myself. Sorry." He looked at his indicators again. Magnetic field strength was off the scale. Radiation levels were as high as during a major solar flare. The error bars in the measurements were at least two standard deviations wide, but whatever the actual figures were, they were high. This thing was pumping out terawatts of energy. The only reason it didn't glow was because it was all coming out as hard radiation. But where was it getting that kind of power? And more importantly, how could they snuff it out before it destroyed the whole damned planet?

He tried accessing the Helios XII research satellite in polar orbit around the Sun, but its signal was just as garbled as what came from Earth. He waited patiently for digital redundancy to fill in the blanks, but even after he built up a reliable reading from the neutrino detector, he saw no unusual activity there. The anomaly wasn't tapping the fusion reactions at the solar core, then.

He looked back at the black amoeba in the visual image, just watching it move. It didn't look real. It was a different kind of darkness than the fathomless black background of space. It looked somehow inverted, like a naked black hole might look if you could see past the event horizon.

He checked the gravitometers again. Nope, no extra mass. But the gamma-ray spectrum caught his eye. It showed a sharp spike in a narrow band he'd seen before, a band characteristic of matter-antimatter annihilation. Could the whole thing be a cloud of antimatter that had somehow drifted into the solar system undetected?

He couldn't see how. It would have hit a comet and flared bright as a supernova while it was still out in the Kuiper belt, or at least glowed like the full moon when it reached the heliopause and started plowing through the solar wind. Space was empty, but not empty enough for an antimatter cloud to slip all the way into Earth orbit without announcing its arrival along the way.

The antimatter had to be coming from someplace else, and there was only one other place that could be: the tension in empty space. Zero-point energy, as it was known in physics. It had been discovered nearly a century ago, but nobody had yet figured out a good way to tap into it because, for all intents and purposes, the stuff didn't actually exist.

The energy came from the spontaneous creation and annihilation of paired particles in free space. It happened everywhere—between the Earth and the Moon, between two falling raindrops, between two whirling atoms—and it happened all the time. The concentration was theoretically infinite, because the energy required to create the particles was given back almost instantaneously when they annihilated one another again, leaving a net flux of zero.

The key was that "almost." For the briefest instant, something new existed in the universe, and $E=mc^2$ no matter how short its duration. And there were so many new particles popping in and out—millions of them every second in every cubic centimeter of space—that at any given moment they outmassed the rest of the universe. Astronomers had finally realized that this was the source of the "missing mass" that held the galaxies together, and quantum physicists suspected that the cumulative instants of duration were responsible for the smooth, linear flow of time itself.

And now David suspected that was where this dark cloud, this hole in space, was getting its energy, too.

He saw a flash on the Earth's surface in the optical image and a spike in the radiation background count.

"What was that?"

"What was what?" Raedawn said. "There are about a bizillion things going on at once."

"Bright flash and hard rads on the ground. About"—he peered at the grid key—"fifty degrees north, by one hundred thirty east."

As he spoke, he called up the political grid. The eastern quarter of Asia popped into place as a ghostly series of lines over the cloud cover; Mongolia and eastern China and Korea stretched out to fit the satellite image. The computer was having trouble fitting Japan's outline to anything in the picture, making false starts and redrawing the lines as various pieces of shoreline appeared and disappeared.

"Juh—Juh—" David had to stop and swallow just to make his mouth work. His scientific composure vanished as he struggled for the words to describe what he saw.

"Racdawn," he finally managed to croak, "Japan is sinking!"

2

R aedawn looked back at her own monitors. "Holy shit, you're right. But that flash you saw wasn't in Japan. That was the Svobodnyy nuclear power plant in eastern Russia."

"Power plants can't blow up," David protested.

"They can if they're running at supercritical to breed weapons-grade plutonium."

"Shit." He knew the Neo-Soviets were arming for war, but he hadn't realized the extent of their treaty violations.

"There goes another one."

David saw another flash to the northwest of the first. Eastern Siberia was going to be a radioactive nightmare for years to come.

But Japan was even worse off. Tidal waves washed in from either side, nearly meeting in the middle, even though the mountains were thousands of meters high.

"Well, what's your theory about this thing?" Her voice broke a little. "I didn't call you down here to gawk at the screens."

"I don't have much of one," David said. "I think it's getting its energy from zero-point fluctuations, but where it came from and what it's doing here are still total mysteries."

She looked at the monitors again, then back at David. "Zero-point what?"

"It's the energy in free space," he said, grateful for her question. He might be helpless to do anything for Earth at the moment, but maybe by understanding how the mysterious nebula worked he might eventually help send it back where it came from. He tried to ignore his horror at so much devastation and just concentrate on the science.

"I think the cloud is somehow tapping into the zero-point field for power. That's why it's so dark; that's actually energy-depleted space we're seeing. The anomaly is using zero-point energy just to exist, which means it's got a temporary deficit to make up, so it's actually sucking *in* anything that touches it. Light, matter, it doesn't care. Anything to balance the books again."

"Is this fact, or theory?" she asked.

"Theory," he admitted. "But a damn good one. It fits everything I've seen so far."

"Uh-huh. Where did it come from?"

He scratched his head and frowned. "That's probably a meaningless question. It's sort of like the Big Bang. It just happened. Space got tangled up somehow and there it was."

She tapped one of her screens, one that showed the Moon wrapped up like a ball of string in the inky black tendrils. "Tangled up is right, but it had to come from *somewhere*, didn't it?"

"Not really. Imagine a rip in a blanket. Where does that come from? Not from outside the blanket. But it's not part of the blanket, either. Think of it that way."

"What's inside the hole?"

"That might be a meaningless question, too. But then

again, maybe not." David turned back to his controls and accessed the NORAD space radar, then waited for the data to fill in.

It was a long wait. Finally, after thirty seconds or so, he realized that microwaves were no better at penetrating the anomaly than light was.

"We may have to send probes in," he said. He looked up at her, saw her looking at him oddly, and said, "What?"

"Are you going to let that thing vibrate all day?"

"Huh?"

"Your communicator. I can see the light flashing from here."

"Oh." David had been so absorbed in trying to think through his ideas that he hadn't noticed. He slid the device off his belt and thumbed it on. "Hutchins," he said.

"Where the hell have you been, Captain?" It was Colonel Kuranda. "I've been trying to get hold of you for over a minute."

"Sorry, sir. I was busy. I assume you know what's happening on Earth."

"Of course I know. That's why I've been trying to reach you. It's time to attack."

"Attack, sir? Attack what?"

"What do you think? The Neo-Sovs, man! Even if Earth survives this, they're not going to be sending us any supply ships. And it'll be a while before we're even close to self-sufficient. Without that, we'll need the Neo-Sovs' infrastructure. We've got to hit them now."

David had to close his mouth, but he opened it right back up again a moment later. "Attack the Neo-Soviets? But, sir, they outnumber us a hundred to one. We're only four squads and we've barely gotten set up. I thought our

mission was to infiltrate and sabotage their colonies, not go
charging in with lasers blazing."

"That was before this . . . this *thing* hit Earth. The entire
picture has changed now."

The colonel was right about that, but David had a hard
time believing that meant everyone should start killing one
another. Kuranda always seemed too ready to fight, but he
was in command of the Mars expedition, and his word was
law.

Despite David's reservations about the general's command style, this mission had been his only ticket to Mars.
The challenge of setting up a colony here had excited him,
even if they had to do it from hiding. As far as he was con-
cerned, Mars was big enough for everyone. David had often
thought that what the two sides needed was a common
enemy. An external threat that would force them to cooperate for everyone's survival.

Adam Kuranda, on the other hand, had been looking for
action since the moment they'd landed. He'd booby-trapped
and completely obliterated a Neo-Sov patrol at the head of
the Valles Marineris shortly after touchdown, and he and his
men were just itching to do it again.

"We still don't have enough manpower for an all-out
attack," David said. "You might be able to take Pavonis or
Tithonium, but they'd just take it back. Or bomb it from
orbit. Either way our colony would be right back where we
started, except that all of you would be dead."

"Thank you for your assessment, Captain Hutchins."
Kuranda didn't appreciate being contradicted. "However, I
only called to notify you in case something goes awry. We
can't just sit on our butts and let our only opportunity evap-
orate. We attack Tithonium Base within the hour. We'll wipe

it clean of troops and withdraw with everything we can carry before the Neo-Sovs can retaliate."

"Dumb strategy," David muttered, though he hadn't meant to speak aloud.

He could almost hear the veins popping out on Kuranda's balding head. "I didn't ask for your input, Hutchins. Stay here and learn as much as you can about that thing that hit Earth. If anything happens that might change our strategic position, I want to know about it immediately. Is that clear?"

"Absolutely, Colonel. And what do we do with your bodies if the Neo-Sovs are kind enough to let us recover them?"

"Good luck to you, too, Captain Hutchins. Out."

David turned to meet Raedawn's quizzical expression. "Well, looks like Kuranda got his wish—an opportunity to kick some butt by attacking Tithonium."

Raedawn nodded. She'd served with the colonel for some time and knew all about his hotheadedness.

"The upside is that either way they'll solve the consumables problem," she said. "If they all go off and get themselves killed, that'll leave only ten of us and a whole base-load of food and recycling equipment. That could keep the few of us going indefinitely."

The notion of playing Adam and Eve with Raedawn held a certain morbid attraction. David had fantasized about it before, for about two seconds at a time. That's all it took before reality kicked in. If he ever made any kind of romantic advance, she would no doubt ridicule him mercilessly and probably emasculate him in his sleep as well. He'd sooner cohabit with a porcupine.

He didn't really think it would come to that anyway. If

Kuranda and his troops got themselves killed, David and the others could always return to Earth.

Provided that swirling black menace from nowhere left anything to go back to. The images from orbit blinked out one by one as satellites died in collisions with its dark tendrils, and ground transmissions grew weaker as the tortured ionosphere filtered out all but the strongest signals. While the footsteps of running soldiers echoed down the lava tube outside and faded into nothing, David and Raedawn were reduced to watching events unfold through the Deimos telescope feed.

They patched sixteen screens together in a 4-by-4 matrix and expanded the view to fill them, then sat and silently watched the destruction. If David let himself think about what he was seeing, the horror of it nearly overwhelmed him, so he found himself noting the unnatural beauty of it instead. Clouds raced across the surface as energy discharges pumped cyclonic winds to jet-stream speeds, and lightning bolts danced from pole to pole, short-circuiting the entire planet's magnetic field and letting aurorae flicker all the way down to the equator. Dormant volcanoes blew. The observatories atop Mauna Kea were now metal and glass vapor in the stratosphere, and Mt. Fuji had lost the top half of its majestic triangular peak as well.

"Jesus," he whispered, repeating it like a mantra as he gradually took in the magnitude of what was happening to humanity.

"I don't think Jesus has much to do with this," Raedawn said, her voice uncharacteristically soft as well.

"I was speaking metaphorically."

"Yeah, right."

Raedawn turned back to the screen, and so did he. It looked like space had been stirred with a broken stick, scratching and swirling it into a multihued mess of darkness and light. As they watched, the image drifted to the left.

"We must have hit the scope's limit of travel," he said. Deimos kept one face toward Mars, but that meant it rotated with respect to the heavens. Earth must be on the horizon from the telescope's point of view.

Raedawn tapped on one of the loose screens on her desk, looked at the readout, then said, "No, it's still got twenty-eight degrees to go. It claims it's still locked on to Earth."

"Let me see that." David took the screen from her and examined the numbers. Right ascension and declination were expressed in solar coordinates. He felt the hair on the back of his neck stand straight up again. "Oh shit," he whispered.

"What?"

"It's tracking the calculated position."

"So?"

"So that means it's the Earth that's moving."

3

The cloud was clearly drawing both Earth and Moon into its grip. David couldn't detect any gravitational effects as far out as Mars, but that didn't mean anything. There was enough loose energy out there to distort space and affect the local gravity gradient. And the tendrils that whipped back and forth across it could be providing impetus, too.

He wondered for a moment if the thing could be alive and consciously devouring planets. Maybe once it was done with Earth and Luna, it would come for Mars and Venus and Mercury as well. He gave that about ten seconds of heart-pounding speculation, then dismissed it from his mind. If that were true, there wasn't a damned thing he could do about it. Besides, Occam's razor said otherwise. This thing was way outside the realm of human experience, but it wasn't doing anything that couldn't be accounted for by physical laws alone. There was no need to invoke a life force to explain it.

Unfortunately, he couldn't think of any way to stop it, either. As the radio signals faded, he directed the telescope to follow the Earth's actual position, but he gained no clues about how to resist it.

Both he and Raedawn fell silent as the doomed planet slipped deeper into the darkness. There were no words strong enough to express the horror of watching their home, and the home of billions of others, being dragged into oblivion.

In a surprisingly short time, it disappeared from sight. The Moon lingered a moment longer, then its gray surface grew darker, as if it were being eclipsed one final time. At last it was gone as well, and all that remained was the roiling black cloud.

"What do we do?" Raedawn whispered.

"I have no idea." David reached out one hand, suddenly needing to touch someone, anyone, even her, just to reaffirm his humanity.

But she looked away to check for any last signals from Earth, and he lowered his hand.

"I should tell Kuranda," he said.

She nodded. Neither of them wanted to acknowledge how pointless it would be.

David used his commlink, and even so had to wait a few seconds before the call was connected due to the scrambling and encryption.

"Kuranda."

"Hutchins. Bad news. Earth has completely disappeared."

"Disappeared how? Obscured by the cloud?"

"More like sucked into it. I don't think it'll be coming out the other side, either."

There was a long silence, then, "Understood. This is it, then. We're on our own."

"Right in one, Colonel."

"Don't worry. We'll get what we need to survive."

David shook his head, a useless gesture over the comm.

"That's not what I meant. Don't you think we'd be better off trying to cooperate?"

"With the Neo-Soviets? The only thing that'd get us would be a knife in the back."

"How do you—"

"Got to go. We're almost there. Wish us luck. Out."

"Luck," David said. He thumbed off the communicator and attached it back onto his belt. Wishing the colonel luck was all he could do to help Kuranda.

Earth he couldn't help at all, but he could at least keep an eye on its killer.

Raedawn hadn't moved. She was still watching the telescope feed, which continued tracking Earth's last-known position. Now it showed only a black splotch against the lesser darkness of space. She wiped at her eyes with the back of her hand.

"Are you okay?" he asked.

"Nobody came out."

"What?"

"Nobody escaped."

David hadn't been thinking that far ahead. Now that he did, that seemed very strange. "*Nobody*? Not from the entire planet?"

"Nope. A couple of ships tried it, but they got sucked in just like everybody else."

"Ships, too! What the hell *is* that thing?" he muttered. To pull in a spaceship, it would have to exert four or five gees of force. That force had to be something other than gravity, because it hadn't pulled Earth that hard. Had it done so, the planet would have broken up like a comet too close to the Sun.

That was a clue. He didn't know what it meant yet, but he would add it to the gigabytes of data he'd already recorded. You never knew what would prove useful in understanding something. That was the nature of research. You observed everything, and with luck and enough data it all eventually made sense.

Of course, it was all academic in this case, unless the cloud did come for Mars now that it had swallowed Earth. He kept checking its position, but it remained where it was. If anything, it was moving slowly away. Or was it shrinking?

He picked up a loose data screen and called up the Helios XII satellite again. It couldn't provide him with as accurate a reading as an Earth satellite, but he could still get a magnetometer reading from it, though whether he could believe it was anybody's guess. According to the satellite, the intruder was now pouring out more magnetic energy than the Sun.

It was definitely shrinking, too.

"Plasma," he said.

Raedawn looked over at him. "What about it?"

"I think it's made of plasma," he said without looking up from the data screen. "Ionized gas so energetic that the positive and negative charges exist side by side in kind of a particle soup. Plasmas are highly sensitive to magnetic fields, and they can also create huge fields when they're in motion."

"Will knowing that help get Earth back out of there?"

He looked up at her, surprised at her angry tone. "No," he said. "I don't think anything could do that. The only way we'll get Earth back is if that thing spits it out again."

"Then what good is all this?" She reached past him and picked up the screen he was looking at. "What difference does it make if it's plasma or ectoplasm? Earth's dead either way."

"I want to know what killed it."

"I want it *back*!" She snarled the word as if it were David's fault her homeworld had disappeared.

"I want it back, too," he said, "but we're dealing with more energy than the Sun puts out. There's nothing we can do to affect something on that scale."

"Then knowing how it works is useless, isn't it?"

"You don't know what's useless. Nobody does." It was an instinctive response. All his life people had belittled him for being a technogeek, for preferring abstract knowledge to the real world, but again and again he'd found practical uses for that knowledge. The more he understood about the way the universe worked, the more he could manipulate its component parts. David couldn't create another Big Bang, but knowing what had happened in the first nanoseconds of the universe's life helped him understand how to tune a fusion reactor. And knowing what had swallowed up Earth might help him learn how to generate that same kind of power for a more practical use. Now more than ever, humanity would need every trick it could muster to survive.

And concentrating on the science kept him from dwelling on the destruction, which could easily turn him into a gibbering wreck if he let it. He couldn't watch Earth get swallowed up by a rogue spatial anomaly and not feel something. He felt plenty; he just couldn't afford to show it. Not now. Maybe not ever.

Raedawn didn't hear all that rationale. All she heard was, "You don't know what's useless." She stood up and flung the data screen to the floor, where it bounced once in the light gravity and spun around on one corner for a second before it landed facedown.

"I know *you're* useless! You measure this and calculate that, but when it comes time to actually do something, you just sit back and watch it happen!" She clenched her fists, visibly struggling for control.

He scooted away and stood up himself. "Hey, I didn't see you doing much, either, but I didn't—"

"Damn you!"

"—accuse you of being a slacker. There's nothing either one of us could have done."

"Well, there should have been."

He slapped the fingers of his right hand into the palm of his left. "Like what? Name something. Tell me, and I'll do it."

She opened her mouth to shout at him, but all she could say was, "You—you—arrgh!" She clenched her teeth and growled like a cornered animal. The sound raised the hackles on David's neck.

"Hey, hey, hey," he said, holding out his hands. "Take it easy."

"Take it easy? Take it *easy*? Earth gets sucked into the void and you want me to take it *easy*? Well, screw you, Mister Rational Block of Ice. Get the fuck out of my comm shack." She took a step forward.

He took another step back. He wasn't about to let her push him out the door. "Come on, Raedawn, I know you're upset, but there's no reason to get mad at me. I didn't do anything."

"Exactly! You didn't do a goddamn thing. So go do something now. Take your precious data"—she turned to the main control console and yanked the continuous memory backup module from its socket—"and go do something useful with it." She shoved it at him, would have punched him in the gut with it if he hadn't stepped back again.

Giving him the backup was a useless gesture since the whole base was networked, but he took it from her outstretched hand anyway.

"Go on, get out of here!"

"All right, I'm going." He sidled past her and walked to the door, then turned around and said, "Look, I'm sorry. I honestly don't know what else I could have done. But I promise if I figure anything out, you'll be the first to know."

She kicked at the screen on the floor. It skittered across the polished lava and banged into one of the equipment racks, still displaying the magnetic field strength as it tumbled. "I don't give a shit if you tell me. Just do it."

David shook his head sadly and stepped into the tunnel corridor, then closed the door softly behind him. His footsteps echoed down the tunnel as he made his way back toward the lab. There was never anybody in this end of the colony, but all of a sudden it seemed even emptier than before. Kuranda and his soldiers were off getting themselves killed for supplies, and who knew where the others were. David wondered if they even knew what had happened yet.

He stopped in the middle of the tunnel and looked back the way he had come. Beyond the comm center, strung out like beads on a necklace, were the administration offices, barracks, and so on. The few people who hadn't gone on the Tithonium raid must have heard the commotion and asked what was up, must have tapped into the telescope feed and watched the same events unfold from wherever they were, but he didn't know that for sure.

If there was anyone who didn't know, David envied them their ignorance. Let them keep it a little longer.

He turned back toward the lab and walked slowly down the corridor, thinking. Desperately thinking, to banish the horror that lurked in the back of his brain. Zero-point energy. Intense magnetic field strength. Plasma. Where did it come from?

Where was it *going*?

The nuclear generator was still waiting for David when he entered the lab. He studied it for a moment, then shrugged and flipped on the power. The base was going to need every bit of equipment functioning at peak efficiency if they were to survive.

He wondered how Kuranda was doing. If the operation succeeded, David knew he would hear about it soon enough, over and over again from every soldier involved.

And if it failed? He tried not to think about what it would be like to cower underground for the rest of his life, hiding from hostile troops while he and the others waited for some vital system or another to break down beyond repair. Life on Mars would be hard enough even if Kuranda and his troops could conquer the whole planet. If they lost their first battle, the survivors could look forward to the life Hobbes had attributed to man in a state of nature: nasty, brutish, and short.

The whole point of civilization was to prevent such savagery. It often didn't, but David preferred it to the alternative. Civilization was humanity's only hope of survival.

The lasers were once again making their six-sided starburst pattern. He checked to make sure the magnetic containment field was switched off—it wouldn't do to have an open fusion reaction only centimeters from his face!—then he leaned in to see the focal point while triggering the deuterium injector.

There was a brief flash of brilliant red light as a microgram or so of deuterium vaporized in the lasers' focus. It flared out in a teardrop shape with the tail pointing to the right; that meant the injector was aimed slightly left of dead center. More of the reactant was being vaporized on that side.

He adjusted the vernier control a few arc-seconds to the right and tried again. Egg-shaped this time. A few more arc seconds and it was a perfect sphere. Just to make sure, he adjusted it farther, and smiled when he saw another red plasma egg with the narrow end pointing to the left instead. He adjusted it back to center and closed the access hatch, sealing off the reaction chamber, then with a grunt from the effort he lifted the lead radiation-shielding collar off the workbench and slid it into place over the top.

When the generator was fully assembled, there would be another shield over the whole works to keep its intense magnetic fields from interfering with electronics, but he didn't bother with that now. He wasn't running anything sensitive at the moment, and there was plenty of rock between him and the comm center to keep the field from interfering much with signals there. Besides, he was only going to test it for a few seconds. Even if it did scramble communications, it would be over before anybody cared. It wasn't like there was anything out there to receive anymore.

The lights dimmed when he switched on the magnets. When the generator was running, it provided its own power, but it took a few hundred kilowatts to get the field strength up to operating levels. He checked to make sure the generator's output was properly hooked into the colony's main bus.

It wouldn't do to have a megawatt of electricity slamming into the system with the wrong polarity. It was correct, though, so he reached out to engage the injector, then stopped short with his hand just above the button.

Black fog was curling around the top of the generator.

The lead collar had turned gray-white with frost. He reached out and touched it, then yelped in pain and snatched his hand back. It wasn't just cold; it felt like it had been bathed in liquid nitrogen!

The black fog swirled outward, growing thick enough to obscure the radiation shield, and a tiny lightning bolt spit outward toward David's face. He flinched back, banging into the workbench. What the hell was this? Were the field coils shorting out? If they were, the whole unit should have melted, not frozen. Besides, he had seen something that looked just like this only a few minutes before, and it hadn't had anything to do with fusion generators.

Or had it? Good God, had the tear in space that swallowed Earth been triggered by Earth's own power stations? He looked at the expanding black cloud around the generator's reaction chamber. Part of his mind screamed *Shut it off!* but he resisted the impulse. If this was the same effect, then it was a golden opportunity to learn what had happened, and maybe even how to reverse it, provided he didn't suffer the same fate as Earth.

He would give it a few seconds at least. Unwilling to risk his fingers again, he picked up a screwdriver off the bench and reached out with it, careful to hold on to the plastic handle. When its silver tip reached the black fog, it disappeared as if he had pushed it into a solid object. He felt no resistance, though. He pushed a little farther, and a little farther, until half the shaft had disappeared. That was absurd; he should have hit the lead shield by now.

He pulled the screwdriver out again and held his hand near

it, then gingerly touched it, but it was merely cold. He rapped it on the workbench. It clanked like a screwdriver should.

He stuck it back into the blackness, shoving it slowly inward until just the handle protruded. It definitely should have touched the shield long before that.

When the commlink at his hip vibrated, he nearly jumped out of his skin. He dropped the screwdriver, which vanished into the dark fog without a sound. It didn't hit the floor, or anything on the other side of the darkness, either.

That was assuming sound could travel through it.

He unclipped the commlink from his belt. "Hutchins." He got a loud burst of static and a barely discernible voice. He pulled the device away from his head to spare his eardrum and on impulse, stuck the communicator into the inky black field and listened. He could still hear the static; it was muted but audible.

He pulled the device out of the darkness and held it up to his head again.

"It's coming for us!" Raedawn's voice suddenly burst through.

He winced. "What?" he asked. "What's coming for us?"

"The black cloud! It's"—another burst, then—"out a big tendril straight toward us."

His mind was still on the phenomenon in his own lab. "The black cloud? You've got one over there, too?"

"Over here? What? Hello, Mars to David. I'm talking about . . . that ate Earth. Big black . . . lots of twisty arms and lightning bolts—remember?"

The magnetic field was interfering with the signal, but not enough to make her unintelligible. "Of course I remember. I'm staring at a miniature version of it right here in the lab."

"You are? How'd it . . . so fast?" Curiosity and fear fought for dominance in her voice.

"It just appeared when I turned on the fusion generator I'm repairing."

"Well turn it off, you idiot! It's attracting the mother ship!"

"I don't think its a spacesh—"

"Now! Turn it off now! It's halfway here!" Fear had definitely won out.

It finally hit him, too. Halfway to Mars already? Holy shit! He reached for the switch, realized that the fuzzy boundary of darkness was uncomfortably close to it now, and pulled back, looking for a screwdriver to flip it with. There wasn't one; he'd already lost the only one within easy reach inside the anomaly.

There wasn't time to waste. Even if this local phenomenon wasn't attracting the big cloud somehow, it was about to engulf the controls, and after that there would be no easy way to shut it off. David transferred the communicator to his left hand and reached out with his right for the emergency cutoff switch. He stabbed at the button and yanked his hand back.

For the briefest of moments, his fingers tingled as if they had gone to sleep. He shook them, then switched the communicator back to that hand. "Okay, it's off," he said. "The field is collapsing."

It didn't go out like a light, he noted. The magnetic field took only milliseconds to lose strength, but the patch of black fog persisted for three or four seconds, slowly growing indistinct and closing in on the top of the generator. It looked as if the radiation-shielding collar was sucking it in through tiny vents.

The gray metal surface reappeared.

"Son of a bitch," he whispered. The screwdriver was stuck straight into it all the way to the handle.

"What's wrong?" Raedawn demanded. "What did you do?"

"Nothing. Has the big cloud stopped?"

"Not yet."

He tried to pay attention to the bigger problem, but it was hard with such a mystery right in front of him. As he reached out to touch the screwdriver handle, he said, "It's halfway here, you say? That means it's about four light-minutes away. It won't know we did anything for that long, and we won't see its reaction for another four after that, so we don't have to panic yet."

"That's easy for you to say. You're not watching it reach straight for us."

The handle was cold, but he could touch it. He gripped it in his left hand and tugged, but it didn't budge. It felt like it had been welded into place.

Something didn't feel right with his right hand. He lowered the commlink for a second, looked at his fingers, and stared in shock at the sight of all four fingertips melting into the plastic.

He yelled "Yaaa!" and shook the device free. His fingers came loose with a wet, sucking sound, tingling all over again, and the communicator flew halfway across the lab before it hit the floor.

Raedawn's voice came out of it in tinny miniature from that distance. "What's the matter?"

"It—" It what? Tried to eat his hand? He had no idea what had just happened.

He picked up the communicator, then quickly set it back down on the workbench. He examined it closely, searching for the marks his fingers must have made in it, but the case looked perfectly normal. There was a scratch along the side where it had hit the floor, but that was it.

"What's going on over there?" Raedawn asked.

He leaned to speak into the communicator without picking it up. "I wish I knew. I've got a screwdriver stuck through the generator core like Excalibur in the stone, and my fingers just slipped into the commlink and out again." On a hunch, he grasped the screwdriver with his right hand and pulled it free of the generator with no more resistance than if he'd been sliding it out of a cantaloupe.

His fingers slid into the handle just as easily. He dropped the screwdriver on the workbench, then cautiously picked it up with his left hand. Nothing unusual happened. The plastic felt normal, and so did the metal blade. But when he pushed it up against the commlink, the blade sank into the case just as easily as his fingers had. He stopped before it shorted something out.

For Raedawn's benefit he spoke aloud as he pondered the meaning of what he'd seen. "It looks like whatever is exposed to the spatial anomaly either gains or loses some crucial quality that lets it remain solid. Except it only reacts with other things that have also been in the field. Very strange."

"What are you babbling about?" Raedawn didn't sound happy.

"Nothing. What's the big cloud doing?"

She didn't say anything for a few seconds, then, "It looks like it's slowing down. It's not pointing right at us anymore, either. Yeah, it's angling away a little bit."

"What direction?" David asked.

"What difference does that make?"

"Humor me. I bet it's moving toward Gemini, right?"

A few more seconds passed, then, "You're right. So what?"

"That's our orbital motion you're seeing. Mars is heading into Sagittarius at the moment, which puts Gemini right behind us. The cloud is reaching for the spot where we were when I shut off the generator."

"Oh."

He pushed the screwdriver into the communicator again, but it was harder this time, and he had to use his right hand to steady the device in order to pull it free. Of course his fingers stuck again, so he had to set down the screwdriver and pull the communicator away with his left hand. He flexed his fingers. They felt normal enough, but he couldn't get over the fact that he had just reached through solid matter with them.

"This is definitely some kind of dimensional thing," he said. "The effect appears to be going away now, but it—" He had a sudden thought.

"It what?"

"Hang on. I've got to set this up so I've got something to study later." He pressed the screwdriver into the commlink's case again, but this time it barely went through. He had to push it straight in, and he misjudged the amount of force needed; the battery socket spit sparks and the earpiece howled for a second, then went silent.

"Well, hell," he said, but he wasn't all that disappointed. Resources were scarce, but magic commlinks with screwdrivers slid into them were somewhat rarer.

He got right to work examining it with a magnifying lens, looking for surface effects where the two objects intersected. There didn't seem to be any; the plastic case didn't bulge outward to account for the extra mass of the screwdriver, and the screwdriver didn't neck down or bend where it entered the plastic. He was willing to bet that neither surface stopped at the boundary of the other; it looked instead as if they had slid through one another right down at the molecular level, their atoms taking up residence in the vast spaces in between one another.

He would have to wait until they had solidified completely before he sawed them apart to see what that looked like inside. In the meantime, he examined the fusion generator. It seemed none the worse for wear. He lifted off the radiation shield and set it on the bench top—noting with relief that his fingers didn't try to slip inside it now—then opened the access hatch to the reaction chamber. It still gleamed bright silver inside.

Out of curiosity, he flipped on the power to the lasers again. They made their familiar six-pointed star, and when he triggered the deuterium injector, the plasma ball was a perfect sphere. He bet if he switched on the confinement magnets, the generator would still work.

Rapid footsteps echoed down the tunnel. Someone was running. Had Kuranda's soldiers returned already? David leaned out to see who it was and saw Raedawn heading toward the lab.

She was out of breath. She stopped just inside the door, her hair sticking out wildly in all directions, her perspiration-soaked T-shirt clinging to her breasts and stomach, her hands shaking as she gripped the door frame for support.

"Are you all right?" he asked her, stepping closer.

"I came as fast . . . as I could," she gasped.

"I can see that. What's the matter now?"

She narrowed her eyes. "That's what I . . . came to find out. I heard a loud *zzzt!* and you went silent. I thought you'd been electrocuted or something."

"Oh. No, it was just the commlink. I accidentally shorted it out. Come look. It's amazing."

"You shorted it out." She took a deep breath, then stood upright. "You stupid son of a bitch, you scared me to death!"

"Oh." He blinked a couple of times. "Sorry."

" 'Oh, sorry,' " she mocked. "You idiotic . . ." She

balled her hands into fists and released them as if she could grasp the words she needed to describe how dumb he was.

He felt dumb. Something wasn't adding up here, but he couldn't figure out what. Why had she run all the way down here just to yell at him? Shouldn't she be relieved that he was okay?

"Come see," he said again, nodding toward the workbench. "It's the strangest damned thing."

"*You're* the strangest damned thing," she shouted. She turned and stomped back out into the tunnel, bouncing high and almost hitting her head on the ceiling with the force of her footsteps.

He stepped to the door. "Raedawn . . ."

"Don't you 'Raedawn' me! Go ahead and examine your precious commlink. While you're at it, why don't you graft it to your stupid head so you don't have to waste a hand while you're talking to people!"

"That's another weird thing," he said, trying to explain to her what was so interesting about it. "It did absorb my fingers for a second. If I hadn't shaken it free, they probably *would* be grafted together by now."

"Too bad you lost your opportunity." She turned to go, but stopped when she got a signal from her commlink. She threw David a dirty look as she thumbed it on and said, "Corona."

What was that all about? he wondered as he turned back to the lab. He could hear Kuranda's voice coming over Raedawn's communicator.

"Mission accomplished, Captain. And I have a little gift for you. State your location."

"I'm at the lab."

"Stay put. Were on our way. Out."

Raedawn looked at David with bewilderment. "We?"

5

avid used the minutes it took for Colonel Kuranda to reach the lab to examine the results of his experiment as Raedawn looked on in cold silence. It was just as he'd suspected; the screwdriver and the electronic gadget had blended right down to the molecular level. He vaguely heard the rumble of booted feet far down the tunnel, but he was so engrossed in his work that he didn't pay any attention until he saw Raedawn snap to attention.

He looked up as Kuranda entered the lab. The colonel's close-cropped gray beard and balding head had always given him a fatherly look. Now, combined with his wide eyes and flaring nostrils, it made him look wild, out of control. Close behind him were two grunts and between them, David was surprised to see a thin, wiry, dark-haired man wearing the uniform of the Neo-Soviet military.

"We got what we went for," Kuranda said. He turned to Raedawn. "Plus we found someone I think you'll find most useful."

"In what way?" she said, eyeing the stranger suspiciously.

The stranger shuffled his feet and looked about nervously.

Kuranda cleared his throat. "He was working in the comm center when we stormed the place. He speaks pretty good English and requested asylum right away. He seemed convinced I was going to execute him on the spot."

Raedawn stepped closer to the man and said, "What's your name and rank?"

The man looked to Kuranda, who gave him a gruff nod. "Lieutenant Boris Ivanov, Communications Specialist. I useful. I can break you into Neo-Soviet comm system."

Raedawn nodded. David knew that so far, she'd had no luck trying to penetrate the enemy system. "There's just one small problem. How do we know he's not a spy?"

"I not go back," Boris said resolutely. "He is crazy man."

"Who?" Raedawn asked.

"General Leonov. He kill people for smallest reason. I am looking for way out for long time. I go gladly. I am tired of war."

Raedawn, David, and Kuranda exchanged glances.

"The troubles won't stop until General Vanivar is dead," Kuranda stated flatly. Vanivar was the driving force behind the Neo-Soviet Alliance. He had reforged its military might through aggressive expansion, lifting the empire out of its long economic slump. And he had no intention of stopping until the entire world was his. Or until he died trying.

Boris shrugged. "Perhaps he is."

The red flush drained from Kuranda's face. Apparently it had only now hit him that the people on Earth weren't just gone, but were very likely dead.

They all stood in silence for a moment. Kuranda struggled to recover his usual hard exterior. "We still won't cooperate with you Russkies. Not after all you've done to us."

The strange conglomeration of fused metal on the work-bench caught Kuranda's eye.

"What the hell is that, Hutchins?"

David walked over and pointed out the screwdriver fused into the circuitry. "It had a little run-in with an alternate dimension. At least that's what I think it was."

"An alternate dimension?" Kuranda asked.

David told him about the fusion generator and the mysterious black fog that had engulfed it when he switched on the containment field. "I think it's the same stuff that ate Earth," he said.

"Is not 'stuff'," Boris said. "Is monstrous." His face reflected the horror of what he must have witnessed at the Neo-Soviet comm center.

"I can either go into hysterics or try to understand what happened," David explained. "Your choice."

"What do you know about it?" Kuranda demanded.

"It's got to be some kind of magnetic effect. It happened right after I switched on the containment field."

He picked up the commlink and held it so they could all see the blended parts. Even the two grunts looked on with fascination. "This transposition effect makes me think it's knocking a hole through normal space-time. I shoved this screwdriver all the way into the generator when it was running, and a few seconds later my fingers slid right through the surface of the commlink even though they weren't inside the field at the time. It looks like anything that's been inside the field loses its definition for a while, and until the effect fades out, more than one thing can occupy the same space at the same time."

"Could it be some kind of alien transporter technology?" Raedawn asked.

"Possibly. It certainly transported Earth and Luna

somewhere. But whoever was responsible didn't seem to care much what shape it was in when it got there." He set the communicator back on the bench. "I'm leaning more toward 'industrial accident' as an explanation."

Kuranda snorted. "All of humanity couldn't muster the energy necessary to warp space to that degree."

"Maybe it wasn't humanity's accident."

Kuranda merely looked at him. The Neo-Sov glanced from one to the other, no doubt soaking in everything he could learn about the Union chain of command as well as the mysterious black cloud. At this point, no one seemed to care.

David continued brainstorming anyway. He said, "What if someone was crossing through the solar system in a faster-than-light spaceship? We have no idea how to actually travel FTL, but all our theories say you'd have to do it through some kind of subspace where the laws of physics are different. That would probably put a lot of stress on the normal space they were flying through. So suppose someone was doing that, and they came a little too close to Earth. Space is already deformed from the mass of the planet, and the Moon stretches it out even more. Add thousands of fusion reactors—some of them not shielded—and you've got a region of space ready to burst at the first disturbance."

"You think Earth was hit by speeding starship?" Boris asked.

"Maybe. It's as good a theory as any."

"What difference does it make?" Kuranda said. "It's gone. That's all that matters."

"Is it?" Before Kuranda could argue, David said, "I don't know for sure what happened, but I've got a pretty good idea how to duplicate the phenomenon on a small scale. The Earth went *somewhere*. I think it's possible to go after it."

"Impossible," Kuranda said. He snatched the commlink off the workbench and held it in David's face, the embedded screwdriver sticking out of it like an old-style antenna. "If you tried it, you'd wind up like this."

"We don't know that. If I'm not touching anything when I go through, there won't be anything to merge with."

"You plan on going through nude?" Kuranda asked. "What about air? When stuff starts mixing together you could get embolisms in the blood, strokes in the brain, who knows what else?"

David was growing exasperated. "Nobody knows," he said, "but nobody's *going* to know unless we do some experimentation. I need to rig up a remote sensor and send it through, see if I can get some data from the other side. See if I can spot Earth, or an alien starship, or something else entirely. If I can bring my probe back in once piece, I'll send a mouse from the biolab, and if that works, we'll see about sending a person through."

"I forbid it," Kuranda said. "You would jeopardize this entire installation and our precious resources for the sake of curiosity."

"I'll do my experimentation in space. I'll go all the way back to where Earth was if you like. That's obviously where the effect is strongest anyway."

"We can't afford to lose a spacecraft, either."

"Bullshit," said Raedawn.

Everyone looked at her in surprise. She'd been unusually quiet up to this point.

"Bullshit," she repeated. "A chance to rescue Earth is one we cannot afford to lose."

"That's true," David said. "You risked more than a ship

today, Colonel, mostly to steal food. One long-range shuttle wouldn't make any difference in the long run to our base."

"If you're determined to die, I can think of better ways to do it," Kuranda said.

"Nobody's going to die," David said. "We're not going to send anybody through until we know it's safe."

"You got that right," said Kuranda. He squinted at the ruined commlink, then set it back on the workbench. "You really think there's a ghost of a chance to bring Earth back from wherever it went?"

David shrugged. "If we find out how it got there, maybe, but I wouldn't bet on it. Like you said, from all of humanity working together couldn't muster the energy to drag a whole planet around. But if we find it, we can at least lead people back from wherever it went. Assuming anybody's still alive."

"Giving us more mouths to feed if they are."

Kuranda paced away from the bench and back, thinking. David knew exactly what was going through his mind. The Union expedition force was hopelessly outnumbered here. With help from home there had been a decent chance for survival, but there weren't enough of them to colonize an enemy-held world. They would be lucky to survive even without the added drain on their resources. On the other hand, the Neo-Soviets controlled Mars and would dominate it forever if the Union expedition didn't get reinforcements from somewhere.

It was a long shot, but as David had pointed out, Kuranda had been willing to risk more just to steal supplies.

After three or four circuits, Kuranda stopped pacing. "All right, here's what we'll do: You and the Russian and Raedawn can take a shuttle back to Earth space." The Neo-Sov jerked his head up in surprise.

Raedawn started to protest, but Kuranda cut her off. "He'll be an asset if you encounter any Neo-Sov ships. Maybe bluff you out of a bad situation. But I want you to be *careful*. No stupid heroics. I want you both back in one piece. We need you here."

Kuranda motioned to Boris and said to Raedawn, "I leave him in your custody. If he gives you trouble, shoot him." Without waiting for a reply, he stalked out of the lab and down the tunnel toward the main colony, with the two grunts close behind.

Raedawn glared at their prisoner. "I still don't trust you as far as I can throw you," she said, "but once we're in space it won't matter. From that point on, we're all going to be working for the same thing."

"Is right," Boris said. "All working to survive."

6

 few hours later, David, Raedawn, and the Neo-Sov were in the shuttle tying down the fusion generator.

David wiped sweat from his forehead. Even in Mars's low gravity, it had been all he and Boris could do to lift the bulky power plant into the cargo hold.

Raedawn was standing in the open cargo airlock among the piles of equipment they had yet to stow. Her black leather jacket once again covered her bare arms and black T-shirt, and she held a gun trained on Boris.

Boris eyed her warily as he cinched tight the wide nylon strap that he had wrapped around the top half of the generator. She eyed him back with equal distrust.

David yanked on his side of the cargo strap. "Let's stow the rest of this stuff and get moving."

Kuranda would only allow them to take a month's rations. He reasoned that they could restock on Earth if they found it, and if they didn't find it in a month, they should give up and come back. Provided they could, of course. If not, it wouldn't matter how much food they had.

It was depressing to see how little room a month's food occupied in the cargo bay. It barely filled one corner. The fusion reactor and a dozen hastily wound superconducting magnets took up another corner, and a magnetometer, rad counter, a half-dozen radar range finders, and a few other instruments took up a third. Weapons filled the fourth; the only pile that David thought was bigger than necessary. However, Kuranda had pointed out that Earth had been headed for global warfare when it slipped away, and that hostilities could still be going on there. If it became necessary to fight their way in—or out—it wouldn't help if they left their weapons at home. Raedawn had agreed with Kuranda, so David had reluctantly allowed them to load missiles, rail guns, assault rifles, grenades, and who knew what else on board.

Of course none of the weapons would work for Boris. They had all been identity-locked. David or Raedawn would have to enter a password before Boris could fire even the smallest pistol, and the authorization would only last for an hour at a time. David wondered how long it would take the Neo-Sov to crack the code if he wanted to, but he wasn't that worried about it. The time to worry about Boris was after he'd learned everything he was going to learn about the Union and about the new phenomenon they were going out to investigate. He had a hunch that moment would be a long time coming.

The more data they gathered, the longer it would be. While Boris and Raedawn mounted missile launchers on the hull, David mounted telescopes, radar, lidar, and a gravitometer. The shuttle already had a telescope built into the navigation controls, but David wanted to be able to see in the infrared, ultraviolet, and radio spectra as well. He had no idea what they might find on the other side or how far away Earth might be when they got there, so he wanted to go in with his eyes wide open.

Assuming they could live through the passage in the first place. To test that, he and Boris, who turned out to have a surprising facility with things mechanical, spent a day assembling a crude spy satellite to shove through the anomaly. While they worked, he'd recounted to David some of the reasons he'd defected to the Union. Hearing about the general who so terrorized Boris that he feared for his life made David think that maybe Kuranda wasn't so bad after all.

At last they were ready to go, and not a minute too soon. The black cloud was shrinking rapidly. The arm that had reached out toward Mars had withdrawn back into the parent mass, and the whole works was swirling tighter and tighter. David had wanted to turn on the fusion generator for a few minutes to see if that would draw it back out, but Kuranda wouldn't allow it. He was obviously afraid it would work too well, and that Mars would suffer the same fate as Earth.

David, Raedawn, and Boris waited for dark, then climbed into their ship and slipped without fanfare out of the cavern on agravs. Raedawn piloted from the right-hand control chair while David navigated from the left. Boris was belted into a chair in the cargo hold. They'd blindfolded him so he couldn't recognize the colony's location through the forward window and also left the dividing door open so they could watch him. David directed Raedawn to fly northwest toward Pavonis, then let her angle the shuttle straight upward and light the drive to send them into space.

There was no artificial gravity on board. The thrust shoved them deep into their seats and forced the breath from their lungs but it let off after a few minutes. The sky turned from pink to violet to black as they rose at a more tolerable one gee into orbit.

"All right," Raedawn said as the red landscape became

a curving wall behind them. "Next stop, the planet-eater. Okay, Boris. You can take that blindfold off now."

"Let's get the satellite ready," David said, unbuckling his seat belt and moving back through the open doorway to the cargo bay. Boris moved to help him.

It took a couple of hours to wire four superconducting magnets to the instrument platform and to tie everything down so the intense field wouldn't yank anything loose. The resulting conglomeration of wires and duct tape looked more like a science fair project than an alternate-universe probe, but David had confidence it would do the job. It was sturdy and simple; the best qualities a remote sensor could have when going into unknown territory.

The plan was equally simple: they would shove the probe out the airlock and activate it from a safe distance. The magnets should provide enough field strength to open the anomaly. Once it had swallowed the probe, they would send a signal to shut down the magnets and power up the instruments. In the event their signal could not penetrate the anomaly, the probe was programmed to perform the same functions if triggered by a loss of signal.

For sixty seconds an onboard camera would do a visual search of wherever it wound up, a wide-band radio would listen for message traffic, and a high-gain transmitter would try to relay the data back through the anomaly to their ship. After sixty seconds, the magnets would switch on again, and the satellite would—they hoped—pop back through the field into normal space.

"What makes you think it'll do that?" Raedawn asked when David described the plan to her. She'd put the shuttle on autopilot and come back into the cargo bay to watch them assemble the reconnaissance probe. "What's to keep it from just sitting there?"

David stopped wiring the bulky magnets together. He hadn't considered that. He had assumed that when you opened a hole in space, whatever was occupying that space at the time would fall through the hole. It had worked that way in his lab, but it didn't necessarily have to happen that way in reverse, did it?

"Good point," he said. "Maybe we should put a rocket engine on it."

"To thrust it where?" Boris asked. "Better to tie rope to it and pull it back."

"Nuts to that," Raedawn said. "I don't want to get that close to it. Like as not, the satellite will pull us in instead of the other way around."

"How about a rocket *and* a rope?" David asked. Both Raedawn and Boris looked at him as if he had spoken Chinese, but he forged ahead. "We've got plenty of missiles. We can deactivate the warhead on one and use it for a tug. The rocket can pull the satellite back out of the field, and we can stand off far enough to be safe if it doesn't work."

"Have you ever tried to pull something with a rocket?" Raedawn asked. "It shoots their stability all to hell."

"So? As long as it keeps pulling on the rope, who cares which direction it goes? Once it's back into our universe, we can go after it in the shuttle."

"I guess that's true enough." She went into the airlock and came back with a 200-meter EVA tether in a belt reel. It was thin as string, but its spun kevlon fiber could hold a fully suited astronaut against five gees of thrust, and rocket exhaust wouldn't touch it. She clipped the belt attachment onto the satellite, then got a Draco launcher and an Arrowhead missile from the weapons stockpile. The missile was a solid-fueled rocket designed for surface-to-surface use, normally launched through a shoulder-mounted tube, but the

Draco could be programmed for booby-trap mode as well. In that mode it would lie in wait until something crossed in front of it, then launch its missile point-blank at the target, or it could be fired remotely with a radio signal.

Raedawn threaded the EVA tether through the back of the launcher and tied it around the rocket's body just above the fins, then slid the rocket into the tube, careful to leave the warhead deactivated. The Draco's computer beeped a warning at her, but she okayed it and put the weapon on standby.

"All right," she said to David. "It's ready to go. We can activate it remotely whenever we need it."

He checked the probe one more time. It had power. The magnets had power. The sensor that would switch on the instruments after the magnetic effects were over had power. The data recorder had power. "We're go here," he said.

Raedawn went forward to the controls again and checked their course. "We're already a quarter million klicks away from Mars. That ought to be far enough for a test."

"Good," David said. "Let's drop this thing overboard and do a little fishing on the dark side."

7

avid wasn't sure the anomaly would open for their probe. He was counting on a repeat of his experience in the lab, but it was by no means guaranteed to work a second time. Intense magnetic fields didn't normally punch a hole through the fabric of space, after all. Now that the anomaly that had swallowed Earth was shrinking, space could be less fragile than before.

Or not. They started with low power at first, just in case. It wouldn't do to create a full-blown planet-eater this close to Mars. The red planet didn't have enough magnetic field to spin a compass needle, but nobody knew how much it took to draw an already-active hole into an alternate dimension.

The rocket launcher drifted at the end of its tether, the cable spiraling out to it in long, slack loops. The probe spun slowly, once every ten seconds or so. David had given it that spin when he tossed it out the airlock. This way its camera and antenna would sweep out at least five full panoramas of wherever the probe wound up. With any luck the cable's drag would make the axis of rotation precess so they would get a complete spherical view.

The three explorers were in the shuttle's control cabin,

watching the telescope image of the probe while David sent the command to power up the magnets. Raedawn had moved the ship about ten kilometers away, but she still waited with her fingers near the engine controls, ready to get them out of there if something went wrong.

"Magnets at ten percent," David said, trying to watch the power gauge and the telescope image at the same time. With the darkness of space as a backdrop, it was going to be hard to see when the field formed.

He gave it thirty seconds before he increased the power. "Twenty percent."

Still nothing.

"Thirty."

Was that a little patch of fog around one of the magnets? He couldn't tell, and after that momentary glimpse he didn't see it again.

"Forty percent."

There were only two chairs in the shuttle's control cabin. Boris was hovering over David's and Raedawn's shoulders so he could see the monitors, his feet braced against the door frame behind them. Now he pointed at the telescope image and said, "There. On the upper right magnet."

Sure enough, an unmistakable tendril of darkness drifted across a silvery patch of duct tape. David waited to see if it would expand to engulf the whole probe, but all that happened was that the other magnets each developed their own separate shrouds.

"Going to fifty percent," he said, pushing the control icon upward to the halfway point.

That did the trick. The black cloud suddenly billowed out and engulfed the entire probe, and tendrils reached outward into space, spitting lightning from their ends. One raced up the tether toward the rocket.

"Oh no you don't!" David muttered, nudging the field strength back downward. At forty-five percent the anomaly stabilized, but it didn't shrink even when he lowered the power back to forty. Either the commands weren't penetrating the fog anymore, or the field was self-reinforcing once it formed.

He sent the command for the magnets to switch off entirely. They should do that automatically anyway in another few seconds, but a little redundancy couldn't hurt under the circumstances. Once the magnets shut down, the camera and radio would power up and start collecting data.

He looked over at Raedawn, then up at Boris. Both of them were grinning. So was he. It was working! At that moment he actually did feel a little like a mad scientist. He had just punched a hole in space and shoved a camera through it. In a few seconds he would learn what was on the other side.

Or maybe in a minute. The transmitter signal apparently wasn't making it through the intense electromagnetic disturbance the field produced.

He watched the clock, his finger hovering over the control to reactivate the magnets. At sixty seconds he pushed the button, even though he knew it wasn't going to work. If the probe's signal couldn't reach the ship, the ship's signal wouldn't reach the probe.

That left the timer. They could tell when it switched on: the dark field crackled with more lightning and swirled a little wider, but another half a minute passed and the probe didn't reappear.

"Looks like you were right," he said to Racdawn. "Go ahead and launch the rocket."

She sent the firing command and there was a bright flash as the Arrowhead roared out of the Draco tube, trailing its line behind it. Then the line pulled tight, and the rocket veered away, tumbled around and shot off at a tangent, tumbled again and came straight for the shuttle. Raedawn held her ground, and sure enough, the rocket swerved away again, jumping this way and that like a fish on a line.

It was an impressive sight, but it wasn't pulling the probe out of the anomaly. The propellant charge finally burned out, and the rocket continued a slow tumbling orbit at the end of its tether, but the probe stayed put.

"Time for plan C," said Boris.

"We don't have a plan C," David reminded him.

"*Da*, but I think I have idea. Raedawn, if you do timing right, you can match velocity with missile as it swings past. I will wait in airlock to catch it. I wrap cable around handhold, and mass of shuttle pulls probe out of muck."

"I'm not taking us that close. Not to the muck *or* the missile."

"Missile is deactivated. Muck has been stable for two, three minutes now. If we drift past with engines off, we make no difference to it."

She bit her lower lip and looked at the telescope image again. David followed her glance. Boris was right; the field hadn't changed since the probe's magnets had turned on. The fact that they were working told him something—the passage through the anomaly hadn't fused everything into an unrecognizable lump—but he would really like to get the camera back and see what it had observed on the other side.

"Let's do it," he said.

Raedawn looked up at him, still biting her lip. "I don't like this one bit."

She turned to Boris. "You going out the airlock like that?"

"Of course not!" Boris leaped through the door into the

cargo section, then shrugged into one of the emergency one-size-fits-all suits hanging beside the airlock. David helped him into it and checked his seals. He watched Boris climb into the pressure chamber, then closed the door after him. There was a whoosh of air, then a thump as Boris opened the outer door.

His voice came through the intercom in the control board. "I am in position."

"So are we," Raedawn replied.

She kept her eye on the monitors, calculating the intercept vector in her head but flying mostly by the same instinct that lets a child throw a snowball at a moving car. The burned-out missile made two more orbits as they approached it, and each time Raedawn corrected with minor bursts of the attitude jets, but as it swung around for another pass she shut down the engines entirely.

"Okay, it should come right up on us in about fifteen seconds," she said.

"Ready here."

They didn't need the telescope image anymore. The space-time anomaly crackled and spit only two hundred meters away, and the expended rocket was clearly visible on its bright white tether as it arced out from behind it.

"Hah, there it is. Come here, come here." They could hear Boris's breath come short and fast. Apparently the sight from the airlock wasn't as mundane as he made it sound. "I think it will fall short," he said. "Move inward."

"No. I'm not firing the engines this close to that thing."

"I will not be able to reach it!"

"Stretch, Russkie. Hook your cable to the handgrip and jump."

"*Nyet!* Jump toward that? You are to joke."

"Then hang on to the handhold and throw your tether reel. Maybe the two lines will get tangled together."

"Not likely." He grunted with effort, then said, "I have jumped. Now you are happy?" A moment later he said, "Caught it. Tying cables together—*yaah*!"

"What? What happened?"

"It pulled me free! My line broke. I am stuck to missile!"

How could that be? David wondered. Those tethers were supposed to hold a fully suited person against five gees or more. The anomaly must have degraded the fiber somehow.

Raedawn laughed. "Let go, dummy. You'll fly away on a tangent, and we'll come pick you up when we're both out of range."

"No I won't! Look!"

They couldn't see the anomaly out of the window anymore; it was already falling behind them. David called up the aft telescope view and ran the magnification down to nothing. Sure enough, there was Boris, looking like a ghost in his white spacesuit as he tumbled slowly *toward* the swirling blackness.

Just then the anomaly reached out a thick tendril toward him. "The probe!" Boris shouted. "Shut it off! Is dragging darkness with it."

"Right." The ship had managed to give it a good tug before Boris's line had pulled loose, but its magnets were still on, generating more field as it moved toward them. David sent the deactivation signal again, but it did no more good than before.

"We've got to go get him," he said.

Raedawn looked at the monitor, then swore. But she powered up the engines again and whirled the ship on its axis, then fired the main drive to send them straight toward Boris. Beyond him, the dark patch roiled and spit lightning, its long, probe-bearing arm slowly reaching out toward him as well.

"You've got one chance to grab hold, Russkie. I'm not making a second pass."

"Believe me, none will be necessary."

The anomaly threw another tendril out toward them, jagged as a lightning bolt, but it stretched out to nothing before it even reached Boris. Raedawn kept them on course, but she turned the ship broadside. "That ought to give you a better chance of finding something to grab on to," she said. "And us a better chance of getting away."

"Hurry," Boris said.

She hit the attitude jets again, firing both the top and bottom sets at the same time to shove them sideways without spinning the ship.

"Five seconds," she said. "Three, two . . ."

They heard a small thump against the hull overhead.

"Oof. *Pashlee!* Go, go, go!" yelled Boris.

Raedawn fired the main engine, and three gees slammed her and David into their seats.

"Are you still there?" David had to struggle for breath enough to speak, and not entirely because of the acceleration.

"Yes, I have arm wrapped around handhold and feet braced, but darkness is following! Go faster!"

The aft telescope screen showed the column of lightning-lit blackness that had followed the probe shooting toward them with phenomenal speed. They would never outrun it.

"No," David shouted. "Kill the engines. We're drawing it toward us!"

"Kill em? You're nuts." She throttled up instead, but a second later saw that it had been a mistake. The cylindrical extension of the anomaly that had followed the probe leaped toward them at least ten times as fast as they could accelerate. She killed the drive the moment she saw what was happening, but it was too late.

"Is going to hit us!" Boris yelled.

David braced for impact. A moment later everything went dark and the ship lurched backward. He couldn't see a thing, but he felt the straps digging into his shoulders and waist and heard things crashing into the bulkhead between the control cabin and the cargo compartment. He had tied everything down against acceleration from the engines, not from getting yanked backward.

"Boris?" he called. "Boris, are you still there?"

"*Da*, I have . . . hold." The intense magnetic field was interfering with his suit radio.

"Can you see anything?"

"*Nyet*. Black as night."

They were definitely inside the anomaly. David's heart was pounding like a trapped creature trying to escape, but he tried to rein in his terror long enough to think clearly. He would need to pay attention if any of them were to survive this. Now, more than ever, they would need every scrap of data he could collect.

He leaned forward, putting his nose right up to the display screens he had been watching a second ago. Nothing. It was as if the photons it radiated never made it across even that short space to his eyes.

"Does . . . does the ship respond to the controls?" he asked.

"Do we want to try?" He heard rustling sounds as Raedawn shifted in her chair. Other than that, silence. The darkness seemed to be swallowing up all but the closest sounds, too.

"What have we got to lose? We're already caught."

"Good point." More rustling sounds, then, "No good."

"I see something," Boris said.

"What?"

"Area of brightness. Growing brighter."

"Which direction?"

"Topside of ship. Straight out."

David reached for the telescope controls, pressing what he hoped were the right command sequences by feel and by memory, then stuck his nose up against the screen again. Yes, there was a feeble glow. Faint and silvery, like the Moon behind a cloud, but definitely something. It was growing brighter.

The heavy backward acceleration eased off. He reached for his seat belt to tighten the straps in case it happened again, but suddenly had second thoughts. "Be careful you don't stick to anything. If this works the way it did in the lab, our bodies might slip right through things until were out of the influence of the anomaly."

"Great," Raedawn muttered. "What else?"

"I don't know." He gripped the edge of the control board with his right hand, then felt the boundary between fingers and plastic with his left. Were they inside the surface, or just on top? It was hard to tell by feel alone.

When he pulled away, he felt a hint of resistance.

"I think we should get out of our chairs. Boris, change your grip every few seconds. And try to float inside your suit with as little contact as possible."

He heard more rustling from beside him, rustling that went on longer than it took him to get out of his own harness. "Do you need a hand over there?" he asked.

"Stay away!" Raedawn snapped.

"All right, jeez, I just asked if—" Then he connected the sound with the situation. "You took off your clothes, didn't you?"

"Got it in one, hot shot. And they came off like warm taffy. If you don't want to be wearing yours for the rest of your life, I'd advise you do the same."

"Shit. Boris! Come inside and get out of that suit. Now!"

"*Da*, sounds like very good idea."

David quickly stripped off his shirt, kicked off his shoes, and yanked his pants inside-out past his feet, then peeled off his socks. The magnifier and electronic multi-tester and Swiss Army knife he kept in his pockets rattled against the bulkhead as they tumbled free, and Raedawn said "Hey!" and slapped something out of the air.

"Wasn't me," he said. He hesitated with his thumbs inside the waistband of his shorts, reluctant to remove that final layer of protection and privacy, but those socks had come off hard. And it wasn't like anybody was going to see him anyway. He gritted his teeth and pulled off his shorts, wincing at the sensation of cloth sliding *through* skin as he did so.

They could hear Boris banging around inside the airlock. "Come on, let's go help him," he said.

He pushed himself to the doorway and bumped softly into something warm and probably very private. He expected a knee in the groin in return, but Raedawn merely flinched backward.

"Sorry," he said. "After you."

"All right." Her voice came from only a few centimeters away. He backed off a bit farther, then after a couple of seconds followed her into the cargo hold.

Boris had already opened the inner door. They had to find him by feel and by sound. David helped him remove his helmet, while Raedawn worked at the wide straps that constricted the suit at the joints to keep it from ballooning out under pressure. Their fingers kept sinking into the fabric and back out again, but David couldn't detect any permanent damage to either. In fact, the effect seemed to be letting up now. It was getting harder to push his hand through things— or to pull the suit's arms and legs free of Boris's skin.

His hands kept touching Raedawn's, and their arms and legs brushed against one another from time to time, but they concentrated on freeing Boris from his suit. The Neo-Sov helped as much as he could from inside, and eventually they got the top half peeled away and went to work on his legs.

A patch of darkness slid against another. David bent close and realized he could see Raedawn's arm. "Hey," he said. "We're getting light again."

"Look behind you," Boris said.

He did, and saw that the doorway into the control cabin was a gray rectangle. "I hope that's a good sign."

"Can you two finish up here?" Raedawn asked.

"Yeah."

"*Da.*"

"Good." A very feminine silhouette moved into the gray light and into the control cabin.

They peeled off the rest of Boris's spacesuit, then his clothes. Neither man spoke for at least a minute, even when they felt the ship spin halfway around. Raedawn was turning it so they were facing into the anomaly. Either she was firing the thrusters manually, or the ship was responding to the controls again.

Then David realized he could see the overhead light. The air looked grainy, like black sand, but he could see vague shapes through it. "The effect is definitely dissipating," he said.

"We must be emerging into normal space again," Boris replied.

"Let's hope." David moved forward to the control-room door and knocked. "You decent yet? I want to look at the monitors."

The door popped open a few centimeters. "I'm not putting anything back on until I know it's safe."

David didn't exactly want to put his clothes on, either, but the thought of letting Raedawn see him in the nude was equally chilling. Under cover of blindness and panic he'd been okay with it, but now . . .

On the other hand, he really wanted to see what the instruments could tell him. Their survival could depend on it. David took a deep breath and moved into the control cabin.

He tried not to look at Raedawn but caught glimpses of pale skin at her shoulders and hips. She seemed to pick up on his discomfort, rolled her eyes, and loosely covered herself with her shirt. But when David saw what was outside the ship, he had no trouble keeping his eyes off her, and he nearly forgot his own discomfort.

There were planets in the distance. Dozens of planets, stretching away above and below like particles in a gas giant's rings. The scale was way off, though. Each particle was an entire world, and there was no central parent body; only ring after ring of alien worlds circling a distant ice-blue nebula that glowed bright as the Sun.

And off in the distance far overhead, just two specks of brightness among thousands, Earth and the Moon glittered like tiny jewels in a cosmic necklace.

8

e found it," David whispered. He pulled himself down into the copilot's chair and tapped at the telescope controls, zooming in until they could see the cloud patterns over the Pacific Ocean. There seemed to be a hell of a lot of storms, but it was unmistakably Earth. They could see the northern coast of Australia peeking up from below and the eastern half of Asia off to the side.

"Can you pick up radio signals?" asked Boris.

Raedawn, holding her shirt against her chest with one hand, reached out to the radio controls with the other. David glanced at her bare back, her vertebrae standing out in shadowed relief, then forced himself to look away.

The radio squealed with interference and hissed with static, but there were voices. Raedawn scanned through the standard comm frequencies, searching for anything intelligible, but most of it was not in standard sideband encoding.

"What the hell is that?" she said softly. "I can't make any sense of it."

David felt a chill run down his spine. Here within a space no larger than the solar system were hundreds of worlds. He wondered what kind of life they might support.

Maybe that had been the point of Earth getting sucked into this other space. Had some superpowerful alien race decided to gather all the sentient species in the galaxy into one place? If so, was it for contact or for quarantine? He didn't know enough to even speculate.

Raedawn narrowed the focus of the antenna to Earth alone, and then she finally got something that sounded like words. David heard "missiles" and a moment later an entire phrase as clear as a bell: "—don't care if they have twenty of them, we're—"

"There," he said. "That's English."

They listened for more, but the signal faded into static.

"Transmit," Boris said. "Tell them we're here!"

"Not yet," said Raedawn. "Let's figure out what's going on here before we announce our presence."

"We probably already have," David said, switching to the aft view. Sure enough, back the way they had come, a swirling white cloud glowed against the gray background. That's why it was black on the other side. All the light it gathered was radiated inward, shining like a beacon for all to see.

Then he realized the scale of the thing. This little hole in space wouldn't be naked-eye visible for more than a few kilometers. It was barely bigger than their shuttle. He zoomed in on a dark shadow in its midst and saw the probe they had shoved through, its tether still dangling off into nothingness.

He wondered if they could follow it home somehow. Part of him wanted to try it *right now*, but another part held him back. Wherever this place was, he and Boris and Raedawn had survived their transit. They had come here to help, not scurry away at the first sign of difficulty.

He looked back out the forward window. "Take us closer," he said.

Raedawn looked over at him for the first time since he'd entered the cabin. He automatically sucked in his gut, then felt foolish for the impulse. Then he was glad he did, because she didn't look away. He watched her try not to stare, watched her lose the battle, and waited for her to say something snide about the cut of his jib. Instead she merely nodded and turned back to her own console.

"Okay, closer it is."

"Wait," said Boris. "We don't know it's safe yet. Things are growing hard again, but—"

Raedawn snickered.

"What is funny?"

"Nothing. You were saying?"

David casually plucked his shirt from where it had drifted against the ventilator grille and laid it over his lap.

"Things not pressed together seem to keep own identity, and effect seems gone now, but under thrust, who knows? Let us wait few more minutes before we try, *neh?*"

"Good idea," David said. He turned back to the telescope controls and shifted the view over to the Moon. Behind it glowed another white cloud, much bigger than the one their shuttle had just come through. That had to be the nebula that had swallowed Earth and Moon. It was smaller now, too small for both bodies to fit through without squeezing much closer together, but it was still thousands of kilometers across.

Near the Moon itself they could see tiny sparks of light flitting across the shadowed craters. "That's rocket exhaust. They still have ships."

"And missiles, too, by the sound of it," said Raedawn.

"I can't believe they would keep on fighting," he said. "Not after getting sucked down the rabbit hole into this."

"That's sure what it sounds like." She turned up the volume and they listened to more static, catching the occasional word. Most of them were meaningless out of context, but there were a few that could only be interpreted one way. "Incoming!" was pretty unmistakable, as was "Fire!"

"Those stupid sons of bitches," David whispered. "How could they do that?"

"They were ready to throw nukes at one another even before they disappeared," she reminded him. "When the black cloud hit, somebody must have thought they were being attacked. And once you start a nuclear exchange, there's no going back until one side totally wipes out the other."

Boris pulled his hand loose from the back of David's chair, then grasped it lightly again to keep himself from drifting away. "Perhaps not. Perhaps they just need example to follow."

"Like what?"

"Like us. We have Neo-Soviet and Union operatives together on rescue mission. Very good evidence that Mars has stopped fighting. If we tell them it has, they would have no choice but believing us."

"Yeah, right," Raedawn said. "If we get too close to our side, I'll be arrested as a traitor, and if we get too close to your side, the same thing will happen to you. *These* guys are still at war." She played with the radio again, eventually receiving a clear broadcast in Russian.

"They've landed troops in Alaska," she said disgustedly. "And we've apparently landed troops in Vladivostok." She tapped the flight controls and whirled the ship around, almost making Boris lose his grip. "Fuck this," she said as she lined the ship up with the white cloud they had just emerged from. "Let's go home."

"We can't just abandon them here," David said. "It's the governments who are fighting. I'll bet the civilians don't like it any more than we do. Probably less."

"The civilians are probably all dead by now."

"They aren't. You can see for yourself that the planet's not in that bad a shape. It's obvious the war hasn't screwed up the biosphere yet."

"Give 'em time."

"All the more reason for us to help them now."

In her agitation, Raedawn had forgotten to hold her shirt against her chest. David tried not to stare as she reached out to the controls to try the radio again, but it was tough. He'd had no idea such a sensuous, feminine woman lurked beneath that brittle exterior of hers.

The voices on the radio pulled his attention back to business ". . . command and tactical forces obliterated . . ." said one. "Medevac twelve to base, we're under . . ." said another.

"Where's the music?" she said. "If the civilians are still alive, where's the music? Where's the weather report? Where's the news?"

"Maybe there's been a radio blackout to keep the Neo-Sovs from targeting the stations."

"Oh, that's encouraging."

"What do you want?" David slapped his hand down on the control console, careful even in his anger to miss anything vital. "The planet's at war, Raedawn. So's the Moon, by the looks of things. They both just got sucked into this— this maelstrom of alien planets, and you're pissed because nobody's playing 'Hava Nageela'?" He lifted his hand, noting that it hadn't stuck to the surface this time.

"Look," Boris said, pointing out the window. David followed his finger and saw a glint of silver against the mottled gray barrier between this place and normal space. It was far to port of the anomaly they had created, and much farther out from the rings of planets.

"What's that?" David asked. "A spacecraft?"

"*Da*, but not like any I ever saw before."

David aimed the telescope at it, and the monitor showed an oblong wedge of polished metal, with three large fins in back and a small canard in front for atmospheric flight. The sides were painted in an intricate pattern of squiggly lines, but it wasn't any form of writing he was familiar with.

"Those are missiles," Raedawn said, pointing at a row of narrow tubes mounted along the undersides of the fins.

"You don't know that."

"All right, then what are they?"

He tried to imagine. They wouldn't be fuel tanks; there were too many of them and they were too small. Nor were they external cargo pods for the same reason. He had to admit that if form followed function, they did look an awful lot like the missiles mounted on the flanks of their own shuttlecraft.

"Maybe they are," he said.

As if to offer proof, one of them leaped away from the silvery ship and streaked toward them. Raedawn immediately fired the engines to move the ship out of the way, but the missile was guided; it simply swerved to follow them.

Boris nearly fell through the door into the cargo hold, but he caught himself on the door frame. "Hide behind cloud!" he said.

"In a second." Raedawn turned the shuttle toward the other ship, activating another control panel on her far right as the ship spun around. The moment the other ship was dead ahead, she slapped the controls three times, and three missiles streaked away toward their target.

"We'll show those bastards a thing or two," she said, firing the engine again and steering them around toward the white cloud. They had to hang on with their hands, since they hadn't strapped down for fear of becoming one with the belts.

The cloud had grown smaller in the few minutes that they had been here. The probe's power supply was wearing out and no longer able to maintain the magnetic field necessary to keep it open. But it was still big enough for the shuttle to hide behind. Raedawn took them toward it at two gees of thrust, spun the ship on its axis with dizzying speed, and braked to a halt just as quickly and shut down the drive before its magnetic core could attract the anomaly. It didn't seem to matter; the anomaly wasn't reacting as strongly to magnetic fields on this side, but it never hurt to be careful.

David kept his eye on the telescope feed until the cloud blocked their view. He watched the incoming missile veer after them and the outgoing missiles flash past it on their way to the other ship. Part of him was furious at Raedawn for firing on what were probably the first aliens humanity had ever encountered, but part of him knew she had done the only thing she could to save their lives. The other ship had fired first.

Was everyone fighting everyone here? Was this place nothing more than a cosmic bug jar where different species were thrown together and shaken until they fought?

"I take it back about the music," he said. "Maybe that *is* a bad sign."

If Raedawn had a comment, she kept it to herself.

They couldn't see if the missiles she had fired had hit anything, but the cloud suddenly billowed out toward them as the incoming one struck it from the other side. Raedawn hit the attitude jets and the nose of the ship dropped down, throwing them into the ceiling but dodging the white-shrouded missile by a couple of meters. The twisted fabric of space churned like a thundercloud just beyond the window.

"Back us out of here nice and slow," David whispered.

Raedawn swallowed hard. "Right."

She pulled herself down into the pilot's seat and this time strapped herself in. She didn't even attempt to cover herself with her shirt again, but the wide five-point harness did a better job of it anyway.

The attitude jets didn't use fusion rockets, so they didn't generate an intense magnetic field. As Raedawn used them to push the ship away, David hovered over the telescope screen, waiting for their first glimpse of the alien ship.

It wasn't long coming. He had half expected to see a dozen more missiles streaking toward them, but instead he saw a dozen tumbling pieces of wreckage instead.

"Woo hoo! We got 'em!" Raedawn crowed.

"Yes, we did, didn't we?" He wasn't nearly so pleased. Earth had been here for over a day, so maybe this wasn't humanity's first alien contact; but it was the first for him, and he had just killed them.

Or maybe not. "Front section seems intact," Boris said.

It did. It looked as if all three missiles had hit in back, probably drawn to the heat signature of the engines. The three wings tumbled away like leaves in a strong wind, and two curving sections of hull spun end over end into the distance, but the long, slender nose of the craft drifted forward without tumbling at all.

David zoomed in on it. There were no weapons ports in evidence, and no suspicious hatches where weapons could pop out from. It looked like Raedawn had effectively pulled their teeth. There was an obvious cockpit set back about a third of the way down the remaining length of the ship. It had two big windows in front and two more on the sides, giving the pilot a wraparound view of space. Either these beings had better eyes than humans or their windows doubled as display screens; no human-built ship would dedicate that much space to an unmagnified view.

Inside the windows, backlit by their own instruments, two long, slender humanoid silhouettes peered outward.

"Now what?" Raedawn asked.

"Is simplest to finish them off and investigate remains," Boris said. "But not best," he added before anyone could protest. "We might learn much from them. We have upper hand; this is good opportunity to try."

"How do you expect to communicate with them?" Raedawn asked.

"Good question," David said. "In all the old movies we blink prime numbers at them, and they let us know when they understand by sending the next one in the series."

"Got a flashlight?" Raedawn asked.

"There's emergency lights in the airlock."

"I get one," said Boris. He pushed himself backward through the cargo bay, flipped end for end, and caught himself against the open pressure door. A moment later he was back with a white plastic emergency light in his hand.

David took it from him, aimed it out the window, and flicked it on and off. He paused, then flicked it on and off twice more. Pause, then three, then five, then seven.

They waited to see what would happen. Nothing. David again flicked the lights on and off in exactly the same pattern. They waited, several minutes seeming to stretch out in time as they ticked by. Then they saw it, a bright green light that blinked back eleven times from the alien ship's cabin.

Communication had begun.

9

Six hours later, the aliens had a better command of English than Boris. They had switched to radio within minutes of exhausting the prime numbers below 100 (for which David was grateful after mistakenly sending them 69), and with telescopes trained on one another they pantomimed motions and exchanged the words for them.

The alien language was nearly impossible to fathom, since it seemed to involve subtle facial gestures as well as spoken words, but the aliens—who called themselves "Kalirae"—seemed to grasp English without any problem. In fact, David suspected there was some sort of telepathy involved, since the Kalirae would occasionally guess at a word that he was sure he had not yet given them. Maybe they had a computer that could extrapolate from root words, but whatever gave them their capability, it was almost spooky.

Their voices were spooky, too. Their vocal apparatus was different from humans'. They had lips and a tongue and vocal cords, but those vocal cords didn't produce the same range. There were overtones that sent shivers up David's spine, like the subliminal sound track to a horror movie. He slowly grew used to it, but the awareness never went away completely.

The humans had donned their clothing again after they were sure it would be safe. Boris had restacked the cargo in back and fixed some food while David and Raedawn played tutor. Now they held up their rations for the Kalirae to see, naming all the parts: eggs, soy cake, cereal, reconstituted milk-like food product. The taller blue one named Gavwin made a repeated smacking noise with its oversized lips when it heard Raedawn call it that.

"We have a similar food," it said. "Tastes very bad."

"You got that right." Raedawn swallowed some and grimaced, then said, "Speaking of bad, why did you shoot at us?"

Neither humans nor Kalirae had broached that subject yet. David winced, expecting the conversation to turn ugly now, but the greenish-gray one named Harxae answered simply, "That is the way of the Maelstrom. Shoot first or die first. After you have been here as long as we, you will understand."

"That's all you have to say?" Raedawn asked.

"No. You won the battle; that should be enough."

"Well, at least you're honest."

"When it is in our interest."

"Right," David said. That, at least, had to be true. "How long have you been here?"

"We must define time units. How much time is this?" Harxae made a soft whistle for a few seconds.

"Do that again," David said, setting his watch into stopwatch mode. When Harxae whistled again, he timed it and said, "That's two point four seconds. We have sixty seconds per minute, sixty minutes per hour, twenty-four hours per day, and three hundred sixty-five days per year."

Harxae and Gavwin stared at each other for a moment, silently communicating, then Gavwin said, "We have been here for two hundred and seventy-three of your years."

"Holy shit," David murmured. "That long?"

"Yes. Even so, we are relative newcomers. The Shard have been here for thousands."

"Have you—I mean, can you—"

"There is no escape," Harxae said.

David leaned forward and looked out the window to the left, where the white cloud surrounding his probe still swirled softly. It had withdrawn the long arm that the Kalirae missile had stretched out of it, apparently drawing the missile back with it, and it had shrunk considerably, but it was still there.

"Are you sure?" he asked. "I'm pretty certain that glow is coming from our sun shining on the part of the cloud that sticks out into normal space."

"You are correct," said Harxae. "But the cloud was dark on that side, was it not? No light from here emerges there. It is a one-way opening."

"It can't be. Look at that cable. The other end is on the other side. If I followed it a centimeter at a time, wouldn't I wind up back home?"

Both aliens were silent for a few seconds before Harxae said, "We don't know. Nobody has ever managed to leave a lifeline before."

"Then let's try it and see before the hole closes," said Raedawn.

Once more the Kalirae silently consulted with each other, then Gavwin said, "She is right. This is a unique opportunity, well worth the risk. I will attempt it."

Raedawn looked like she might protest, but after a few seconds she merely said, "Go for it."

David reached out and turned off the radio for a second. "Do we want a potentially hostile alien poking his head into our solar system?"

"Do you want to climb up that rope first?"

"No."

"Me either, not if somebody else will do it. But if he makes it, I'll be right on his tail. Armed for bear. No offense, Boris."

Boris laughed. "None taken."

David bit his lip, then said, "I guess that makes sense." He switched on the radio again.

"—will trail another line so you can pull me out if necessary," Gavwin was saying.

"Right. Don't actually pull on the cable that goes through the hole; it's not attached to much on the other side."

"I understand."

The blue Kalira disappeared from view into the back of their ship, and a few minutes later an airlock door slid aside and he emerged in a spacesuit. It was skintight, like a plastic bag just half a size bigger than his body. He was half again as tall as David, but no heavier, which gave him a thin, stretched appearance even in his suit. He held a long, coiled tether in one hand, which he threw out into space. In his other hand he held a reaction pistol. He jumped toward the white cloud, corrected his course with the reaction pistol, and drifted into the billowing surface.

"Growing dark," he said. "Cannot . . . cable. I will . . . " The magnetic effects were breaking up his signal.

They waited for him to say anything more, but minutes ticked by with no word. His lifeline jerked once, then stopped. He wasn't making progress. Was he still trying to find the cable, or had he reached it but was just having trouble following it?

Then an eye-searing bright light flared within the white cloud, blasting it into shreds of fog. For just an instant they could see a normal star field where it had been, then the gray veil of the maelstrom's edge rushed in to seal the breach.

"*Chort!*" Boris exclaimed. "He hit missile."

"Arrrrrada!" Harxae howled in anguish.

David had no idea what the word meant, but the sentiment was clear. He wished he had words of consolation for the alien, but he couldn't spare the time to think of it. His hands flew over the controls, examining the magnetic field, optical and radio wavelengths, radiation count, and tracking the debris that flew away from the explosion. If he could get the specs on that missile from Harxae, he could use the ejecta's trajectory to calculate how much energy from the blast had been absorbed. That would give him an idea how much had gone into opening the hole.

Already his mind was awash with questions. Was it the shock wave that had done it, or the intense light, or something else entirely? What if they launched another missile at the spot where the hole had been? What if they hit it with a flare? How about a laser? There were a million things to try.

He glanced upward along the ring of planets. Off in the distance glowed the even bigger anomaly that had delivered Earth into this unlucky place. If it persisted long enough, there might actually be a chance to send the planet home.

Then another thought hit him. "Is there any chance Gavwin could have survived that?"

"You're kidding," Raedawn said.

"He's alien. Harxae? How about it? How tough are you guys?"

"Very tough," the Kalira answered, "but not strong enough to withstand that. Gavwin has ceased."

So the aliens could be killed. Much as it disturbed him to think like Colonel Kuranda, it looked like a military attitude might be even more of a survival skill here than it had been back home.

All the same, a little compassion never hurt, either. "I'm sorry," he said. "We shouldn't have been in such a hurry to try an untested theory. We need more information before we make another attempt to leave this place."

"That would be wise," said Harxae.

David heard the pain in the alien's voice.

"Did he have family? Should we notify his next of kin?"

"All who care already know of his passing."

David wondered if that was because of some telepathic link within their species, but this didn't seem like the time to pepper Harxae with questions. If anything, it was time to make what amends they could and hope for better relations with the Kalirae than what they'd started out with.

"Your ship is crippled," he said, "and we're way out of our element here. Why don't you come with us to Earth? With your knowledge of this place you might be able to help us save some lives there, and maybe together we could figure out a way home for all of us."

"That is unlikely," said Harxae. He looked out the window of his damaged ship at the humans, his expression unreadable even in the telescope view. At last he said, "But new races bring the only hope we have in this place. Eventually someone must come up with a theory that will let us understand it. Perhaps it will be you."

"I've got a few ideas," David admitted.

"Then by all means, let us explore them."

Raedawn didn't bother to switch off the radio. She just said straight out, "Wait a minute. This guy tried to kill us just a few hours ago. I don't mind talking to him now that we've disarmed him, but do we really want him on board our ship? Or on Earth?"

"Gavwin died for you," Harxae said.

"Bullshit. Gavwin died for you, and for the rest of the Kalirae."

"You were quite happy to see him take a risk that might benefit you."

"Of course I was. But that doesn't alter the fact that he did it for his own self-interest."

Harxae said, "As I told you before, that is the way of the Maelstrom. If you intend to survive, there are two rules you need to remember at all times: everyone is out for themselves, and the weak die first."

"That just reinforces my case," said Raedawn. "We'd be stupid to bring you on board."

"It would be a risk," Harxae acknowledged, "but David is right when he says that I could help save many lives on your home planet. For instance, I know some of the races you will soon encounter. I know their strengths and weaknesses and how to make them allies or enemies. You must decide if that is worth the risk of bringing me on board."

Raedawn snorted. "What's in it for me?"

"Raedawn!" David said.

"Hey, I'm just following Harxae's rules. If everybody's supposed to be out for themselves, what's my own personal advantage in bringing a potentially hostile alien on board my spaceship?"

David looked at Boris, who spread his hands out in a "who me?" gesture.

If Harxae was offended, he hid it well. "You learn quickly. Good. Very well, I will teach you to kill."

"Kill what?" asked Raedawn.

"Everything but me."

10

David and Boris both held pistols on the Kalira as it came through the airlock. David hoped the threat would be enough to ensure good behavior, because he wondered if he could shoot an alien point-blank even if the creature seemed dangerous.

He had the same misgivings about Boris. He had hesitated about giving the Neo-Soviet a live weapon, but he needed the backup. Raedawn had a pistol, too, but he wanted her up front to defend the controls in case things got ugly back here in the cargo hold. It was a calculated risk. Boris's gun would only be good for an hour, but by then they would have a much better idea what they faced.

The Kalira had to bend nearly double to fit through the door, and it couldn't stand upright even in the cargo bay. David thought that ought to slow it down a bit in a fight, but he remained cautious just the same.

"Welcome aboard," he said when their guest had removed its helmet.

"Thank you. Here is my food. It need not be kept cold." Harxae handed over a net bag full of plasticlike containers and glittering gold foil boxes, all of which had a bizarre sheen to them. It must have massed at least a hundred kilos altogether; David shoved it into a corner against the back wall with his feet while he braced himself against the side wall with his hands, then wrapped a cargo strap around it to hold it in place.

Up close, the Kalira looked even more stretched out than it had through the intervening space between ships. It was easily two and a half meters tall, its arms reached all the way to its ankles, and its legs were longer than a super-model's. David could have encircled Harxae's waist with his fingers; Harxae could have encircled it twice and had an extra joint of overlap. Its bald head was a half meter oblong, its greenish hue giving it the look of a melon or a zucchini, but it did at least have humanoid features. Two eyes beneath a wrinkled brow, a long, aquiline nose, one mouth, and a pointed chin. Its ears were afterthoughts, but they were in the right place.

A pendulous loincloth hung from its waist like beard moss from a tree, scrunched up now inside its clear space-suit. That was its only clothing, but it didn't look like it needed more; the rest of its body looked hard as polished stone. A round pendant that looked like hammered copper hung around its neck. It was etched with some sort of sym-bol, a web of intersecting lines.

David found himself thinking of Harxae as "he," but that was more from the lack of feminine features on its bare chest than from any positive masculine features. Its loin-cloth hid any more obvious gender marker, but David real-ized he couldn't think of an intelligent being as "it," and there was nothing about the Kalira to suggest femininity. He made a note to ask about gender when the time was right, but this moment of armed reception was not that time.

"Have you got any weapons?" asked David.

"None that I can remove." As if to illustrate, Harxae peeled out of his clear spacesuit and handed it to Boris, who put it with his bag of food.

"What do you mean, none that you can remove?"

"As you suspect. I am telepathic. That ability can be used to project thoughts as well as receive them. I cannot take over your mind nor even speak to you directly, but I can sometimes distract an opponent with an emotion. The effect often gives me an edge in battle."

David wondered if that was all it would do. If he were in Harxae's shoes, he wouldn't give away all his secrets.

Harxae picked up on his thought. "If I had intended to harm you, you would already be dead. Trust me or kill me."

David's instincts told him the Kalira was friendly, but could he trust his instincts around a telepath?

"I'll trust you for now. But don't try anything, and pray that I don't have any sudden mood swings."

"Understood." Harxae stretched out diagonally in the cargo hold. It looked a little like a crane reaching out from a space station to grasp a ship for docking, but Harxae merely floated there, feet oriented toward the back wall. "I am ready to go anytime you are."

"Right." David backed up and rapped on the closed door to the control cabin. "All set back here."

"All right," came Raedawn's muffled voice. "One gee in ten seconds."

David and Boris took up positions in the corners as far from Harxae as they could in case the alien tried anything while they were under thrust. David counted down the seconds in his head, inevitably counting too fast, and was just opening his mouth to say, "What's wrong?" when the engines lit.

Sudden weight shoved them to the deck. Both men,

used to Mars's lighter gravity, grunted with the effort to remain standing, but Harxae took it as if nothing had happened. The thrust went on for long minutes as Raedawn built up speed, then she slid the door open a crack and said, "Free fall in ten."

"Roger," said David. When the thrust ceased, he let the tension in his legs send him forward to the control cabin door. Raedawn had let it slide a hand's-width into the bulkhead; he grasped its edge to stop himself and asked, "How long do we coast?"

"Three hours."

"Don't count on that," Harxae said. He hadn't moved any nearer, but his height already put his head close to the door.

"What?" Raedawn asked.

"Things are not always as they seem here. Space itself is different. There are currents and eddies everywhere, but especially near planets that have recently arrived."

"You're saying there might be some kind of shortcut between here and there? In clear space?"

"Yes. Or a long cut. That is equally likely."

"Is there any way to detect them?"

"None that we have discovered."

"Great."

David didn't know whether or not to believe him. There was no good theory to account for the phenomenon he described. Wormholes, maybe, but this didn't sound like wormholes. It sounded like two different kinds of space, like ether and phlogiston mixing together in some nineteenth-century scientist's lab. Or not mixing, by the sounds of it. If the effect was strongest around new arrivals into this place, then it could be the result of ordinary space not blending with whatever dimension this was.

Except ether and phlogiston were both imaginary quantities, their existence disproven years ago. Space was space, isotropic and homogeneous in all directions. There was nothing to mix.

At least not in the universe David knew. If this was a different universe, all bets were off. A universe born of a different big bang could have different physical laws. It probably *would* have different physical laws. Things like the speed of light and Planck's Constant were determined by chance during the first nanoseconds of creation; the odds that they would be the same in two separate explosions were unlikely at best. And every change would have repercussions all through the physical world. A different Planck's constant would change the energy density of free space, which would affect the curvature of that same space, which meant pi might be larger or smaller depending on which way it curved. It might even be a rational number here.

On a whim, he tapped his wristwatch into calculator mode and called up pi. The display read 3.1415. He did it again and got 3.1414.

"What the—?"

"Something wrong?" asked Raedawn.

"I think the magnetic effects of passing through the anomaly must have tranged my watch. Use the main comp to calculate pi for me, would you?"

She tapped at the controls, and a moment later said, "Three point one four one three two five."

David had recalculated it the moment she did, and that's what his watch said, too. "Son of a bitch. They couldn't both be wrong exactly the same way. That means the value is really shrinking. Space is growing more curved."

"*Vi shotetye!*"Boris said. "Your watch doesn't actually

measure pi. Is calculation. Mathematics is same everywhere, *nyet?*"

"Apparently not." David ran the calculation one more time and said in amazement, "It shouldn't work this way, but it does. I can't explain it." He tried to imagine what would happen if space were curved more tightly. If pi was smaller, then the circumference of a circle would be smaller as well, compared to its diameter, and since any path in space was actually a segment of a cosmic great circle . . .

"We're going faster than we think we are," he said. "Watch out we don't overshoot."

He looked at Harxae, not even trying to hide his smug expression, but if the alien was impressed, he sure didn't show it. He should have been, though. David had solved in ten minutes something that had stumped the Kalirae for over two hundred years.

Sure he had. He didn't know much about these aliens, but they were smart enough to stumble across a changing physical constant. Which meant Harxae knew how to locate spatial anomalies. The alien had been holding back.

And with telepathic ability, he also knew that David knew he'd been holding back, and so on ad infinitum.

"Did I pass your little test?" he asked.

"Admirably," said Harxae.

"What else are you hiding from us?"

The Kalira held his hands together at the base and spread his long fingers out wide. "Many many things. More, even, than you are hiding from me."

"That's no surprise, if you're reading my mind."

"Perhaps I should have lied to you about that? Yes? No?" He lowered his hands. "Communication is easy. Trust takes longer. We will eventually share all we know. Be patient."

David snorted. "You may have found the concept in our language, but patience is not a human virtue."

"Perhaps you should try it sometime."

"What for? So we can wait around inside this planet prison for what was it—two hundred and seventy-three years? No thanks." David nodded toward the pile of electronic equipment in the corner of the cargo hold. "I plan to bust us back out of here just as soon as possible, with or without your help."

11

They were halfway to Earth when Harxae said to Boris, "Your weapon is useless now."

Everyone glanced at the Russian's pistol, which he still held loosely in his right hand. The power indicator glowed green, but now there was a tiny red light beside the security lock plate. David felt a momentary rush of adrenaline at the thought that he had no backup if Harxae suddenly attacked, but the Kalira sat impassively in the airlock, folded up his knees next to his head to be out of the way during the free-fall portion of their flight.

Boris flipped the pistol to David, who caught it left-handed, thumbed the lock plate, and handed it back. The security light blinked until Boris thumbed it himself, then it went out.

"Thanks," he said, but whether he was talking to David or Harxae was unclear.

It seemed pointless to continue guarding the alien at gunpoint when he could apparently read their minds well enough to know when they would or wouldn't shoot, but David didn't know what else to do. The way Harxae treated everything like a test, he might feel obliged to take over the ship if they gave him the opportunity.

Things had seemed so much simpler back on Mars. He hadn't expected it to be easy to follow the Earth through an interdimensional rift in space and bring it back home, but he hadn't factored in trying to deal with hostile aliens—maybe hundreds of species of them—in the process.

Raedawn was still in the control cabin with the door cracked open just enough to listen in on the conversation in back. David heard her combing through the radio frequencies again, searching for a clear signal.

"So what's this place for, anyway?" he asked.

Harxae didn't need to ask what David meant. He said, "No one knows, but theories abound. Some think it's divine retribution for their wrongs. Others think it's a test. Others think we've been put here merely to entertain the makers with our struggles."

"The bug jar theory."

Harxae tilted his oblong head and squinted in concentration. "We do not have 'bugs' on our world, at least not as you know them, but I understand the concept. My own personal theory is that we are put here to rid the galaxy of us, so the makers can live there in peace. It can't be coincidence that every race brought here is warlike, or that they all were poised to spread beyond their home planets when disaster befell them."

"Maybe it is," David said. "I discovered that intense magnetic fields will open a gateway into here. Spacefaring races at war would be manipulating all sorts of magnetic effects. Maybe this is just where you wind up if you twist space a little too tightly."

With iron certainty in his deep voice, Harxae said, "No. There is malevolent intent. I can feel it."

David wondered if he meant that literally or figuratively, but he didn't pursue it. Either way, it was a subjective impression. "Okay," he said. "Assuming there is, have you got any idea who's behind it?"

Surprisingly, Harxae said, "Yes. There is evidence of a race even older than the Shard, a race we simply call the Ancients, who had powers far greater than any in the Maelstrom today. What few artifacts of theirs we have been able to recover show a mastery over space and time that we have never been able to achieve, or even fully understand."

"And you think they created this place on purpose."

"Either them, or someone even more powerful than them. The Ancients may have been stuck here just like the rest of us."

Boris had been listening quietly all along. Now he said, "If that is true, then we are here for eternity."

"No" said Harxae. "Even the Shard will not be here for eternity. The Tkona is always hungry."

Knowing he wouldn't like the answer, David nonetheless asked, "The Tkona?"

"Surely you noticed it. At the center of the rings, the blue-white nebula that passes for a sun here?"

"I saw it."

"It is not a sun. It may be a black hole, but if so, it is no ordinary black hole, either. There seems to be no event horizon. Light pours from it, and tendrils of energy reach out from it to snatch planets at random from the rings. Gravitational anomalies abound. The inner worlds sometimes fall out of orbit and drop straight into it in a matter of hours, and even the outer worlds inevitably drift inward."

Harxae's tone of voice grew soft. "The Kalirae have been lucky. We've managed to stay in the outer ring, but those who fall inward seldom survive more than a few years."

"That's encouraging."

"Ah, sarcasm. How refreshing. Humor is the first thing to die here, it seems."

Boris said, "I will tell you joke about the academician and the *bezabrazny* babushka. There was this ugly old woman, you see . . ."

David heard Raedawn's voice in the control cabin, so he pushed the door into the bulkhead and stuck his head in.

She was talking to someone over the radio. "Montana?" she asked. "Why there?"

"Security," said a thin voice, shot through with static. "The Neo-Soviets have already nuked Seattle and Detroit, and they've got fighters in the sky and in space all around us. Right now the middle of the continent is the safest place to set down."

David felt the hair stand up on the back of his neck. The people of Earth had dropped nukes in the middle of all this? The world had gone insane.

"Who are you talking to?" he asked.

She switched off the microphone. "Union Space Command."

"Did you tell them who we're bringing with us?"

"Yep. I think that's why they want to make sure we get down okay. They're sending out an escort just to make sure. Apparently the Neo-Sovs are shooting at just about anything that moves, above or below the atmosphere."

"Good," David said. "About the escort, I mean."

He turned back into the cargo hold, only to see Boris holding his pistol pointed straight at his own head. "Take ship to Cuba, or Russian gets it," he said.

"*What?*" David raised his gun. Boris's mind was obviously under Harxae's control, but he didn't know what to do about it. Shoot Boris? There would be no more point in that than letting the man shoot himself. Shoot Harxae? But he didn't know if he could kill the Kalira before he made Boris pull the trigger. He held the gun on the alien anyway and said, "What the hell are you trying to pull?"

He heard Raedawn duck to the side to be out of the line of fire, then draw her own pistol from its shoulder holster under her jacket.

"Nothing!" Harxae said, holding his hands out in what was apparently a universal gesture of appeasement. "I'm not influencing him."

"I'm supposed to believe he'd hold a gun to his own head?"

Boris laughed uproariously, then lowered his pistol. "Who do you think invented Russian roulette? I grow tired of pointing guns at one another, so I make little joke to lighten mood, is all."

"Little *joke*?" David said. "You call that a joke?"

Harxae said, "David could have shot me!"

Boris looked from David to Harxae, his brow furrowed in puzzlement. At last he said, "You're right, sense of humor is first to go."

"If that's what you call funny . . ." David growled. "Give me that gun."

"Oh, come now, I meant nothing by—"

"Give it here!" David held his own weapon pointed straight at the bridge of Boris's nose. The Neo-Sov locked eyes with him, staring him down, and at that moment David realized his mistake. If Boris didn't obey, David would either have to shoot or lose what little authority he had over him. He couldn't even blink, or Boris would know he had won the battle of wills.

Boris could blink. He did, even glanced at Harxae. But he couldn't look back. David watched him try, his face quivering with the effort to move his head—or even just his eyes—but he was frozen into place.

Then, slowly, he stretched out his hand and let go of the gun. It pinwheeled slowly through the cargo hold, right past Harxae, who could easily have plucked it out of the air, but neither Boris nor Harxae moved until David had caught the gun clumsily in his left hand and passed it behind him to Raedawn.

"All right, you can let him go," he said, noticing a swirling pattern of light around the pendant hanging down the alien's chest.

"He will recover on his own in a few minutes," said Harxae.

"What *is* that thing?" David asked, motioning to the pendant.

"A symbol of my race. It also has . . . certain powers."

"I can see that," David said testily. He was kicking himself that he hadn't thought to check the talisman when Harxae first boarded. It could've gotten them all killed. Of course, the fact that the alien hadn't used it until now was some confirmation of David's uneasy trust.

"Give it to me," David said. He was both surprised and relieved when Harxae took off the pendant and held it out to him. David half expected to feel a jolt when he touched it, but it only felt like a small cold piece of metal. He put the pendant in his pocket.

He turned back to Boris, who didn't jerk free all at once. His eyes slowly came unstuck, then his head, then his limbs. He raised his arms out before him and flexed his fingers, making sure they all worked, then clenched his fists a time or two. David waited to see what he would do. He expected an angry outburst, maybe even a physical assault, so he wasn't ready for Boris to pull his knees up to his chest, wrap his arms around them, and howl with anguish.

"What? Boris?" He tucked his gun into his belt, thought better of that, and handed it to Raedawn to add to her collection, then pushed himself across the open cargo bay to where Boris floated, shaking with emotion.

"Boris, are you all right?"

"No," he said. "I am not all right! Yesterday I simple communications specialist. Now my country in all-out war with yours, our homeworld has fallen—literally—into chaos, I have lost Mars, my rank, my nationality, to become second-class citizen in your Union, and now even our prisoner can control me like puppet. Why should I be all right?"

"When you put it like that . . ." David said, awkwardly putting an arm around the other man's shoulders. He decided not to tell him about the nukes just yet. "I'm sorry. We've all had a rough day, and I suppose I haven't made it any easier."

Boris didn't acknowledge his touch, but he didn't flinch away, either. David wished Raedawn were doing this instead of him, but at the same time he was glad she wasn't. She would probably just tell Boris to get over it. Or worse.

"We're landing in Montana," he said. "The top brass there is pretty eager to meet you. And you," he added, nodding to Harxae.

"No doubt so they can interrogate us," Boris said.

"I'm sure they'll want to debrief you."

"It's not the questions I'm worried about. It's how they'll ask them."

David let go of his shoulder. "You won't be harmed, Boris. Colonel Kuranda didn't give you any trouble, did he?"

"He had no time."

"We'll tell them you've requested asylum. Everything will be fine. You'll see."

Harxae murmured something too soft to hear, then said in a voice that held a note of surprise, "Foolish as the practice seems, I sense the truth in his words."

David straightened up and looked at the alien. "You think we should strap you to a chair and zap your feet with electricity until you tell us everything you know?"

"Yes, you probably should, though I am grateful to learn that you won't."

David wondered if that meant that the Kalirae would torture information from him if the roles were reversed, but then he realized there would be no need for them to do that. They could simply read whatever they wanted to know straight from his mind.

He crouched down next to Boris again. "Look, I'm sorry. Things look pretty lousy right now, but they're bound to get better."

"What makes you think so?"

David slapped him on the back. "Because they can't get much worse."

"Uh-oh," said Raedawn from the control cabin.

David instantly regretted his words. He wasn't superstitious, but the universe certainly did seem to take perverse delight in punishing foolish optimism. He looked to Raedawn, who was focused on the controls, and she looked as tense as a wire.

"Raedawn?" he asked. "What's the matter?"

"Our escort is under attack. Brace yourselves for maneuvers. We're going to have to try to get through on our own."

12

avid jumped for the control cabin, pulled himself into the copilot's chair, and strapped in. A side-lit Earth filled the view through the windows, but the telescope screen held the action: against the dark side of the planet two ships spat bright flame under hard acceleration, one pursuing a third ship that was arcing around to avoid them, the other coming straight on. An expanding cloud of gas and debris behind them showed where a fourth ship had already failed to dodge a missile.

"How's our armament?" he asked.

"We've got three shots left."

That's how many she had launched in one burst at the Kalirae. "Not good. Have we got time to reload before you boost?"

"No. But if Boris can get suited up now—"

David turned halfway around in his chair. "Hear that, Boris? Suit up and get ready to reload our missiles. Please."

Boris had recovered some of his aplomb. "*Da*. Harxae, toss me suit from there beside airlock."

The alien found it for him, then began pulling on his own suit.

"Thrust in five, four, three, two, one," Raedawn said.

Weight slammed them backward, way more than Earth normal. She was pouring on the gees, trying to build up velocity so they would be harder to hit and harder to catch if they made it past the approaching Neo-Soviet ship.

"Slave the missile controls to my side," David said. "You can fly, and I'll shoot."

"All right." Raedawn's fingers danced over the weapons panel to her far right, and the screen directly in front of David lit up with the tactical display. He checked the stats on the craft that was coming for them: range, 15,000 kilometers; relative velocity, 25,300 kph; accelerating at 3.5 gees. With their own acceleration added in, their courses would intercept in . . . call it ten minutes, but the battle would be over long before then. Missiles accelerated at ten gees or more.

Plus there was the curvature of space to consider. If there were any fast or slow spots between the two ships, that would make accurate targeting impossible. The missiles would have to rely entirely on their onboard homing devices.

He checked the value of pi again: 2.8604. Space was *tight* here.

"I think we should coast," he said.

Raedawn looked over her left shoulder at him. "Why?"

"Because there's no way in hell they can hit us ballistically with the physical constants of space as mixed up as they are around here. And if we shut down the engines, they can't track our heat signature."

"That still leaves radar. We've got a radar cross section as big as a truck."

"So let's give them something even bigger to shoot at."

David swiveled partway around and said to Boris, "Screw the missiles. Toss out live radar beacons."

Boris was still struggling to get his spacesuit over his shoulders. "We *have* beacons?" he asked.

"Not designed as such, but we've got half a dozen self-powered range finders. They put out a hell of a signal. If you aim them at the oncoming ship when you toss them out, the missiles will go for them instead of us."

"That might work," Raedawn conceded. She shut down the engines, and their weight slipped away again. "Okay. Get on it. They're coming up fast."

"How many should I set out?" Boris asked.

David tried to guess. How many shots would the Neo-Soviets take at them? He looked toward the two other ships, one Union and one Neo-Sov, but they were already disappearing around the curve of the planet. Neither one of them would affect the battle here. "Toss 'em all," he said. "We can get more on Earth."

"Right."

Harxae said, "I can help release them."

"Go for it," David said. He got up and helped Boris dig the radar units out of the pile of electronic equipment while Harxae finished putting on his suit.

"Five minutes to contact," Raedawn called. "Less than that for missiles."

"Time to do it," David said, shoving them both into the airlock.

"I may be able to help more if you will give me back my talisman," Harxae said as he squeezed in. On impulse, David took the pendant out of his pocket and shoved it into Harxae's hand. If the alien had wanted to kill them, he'd have done it by now. And they needed all the help they could get.

It was a tight fit, but Harxae bent nearly double and Boris leaned over the six suitcase-sized radar units, which let them get the door closed. A moment later the air rushed out, and the outer door opened.

David went back to the copilot's seat, buckling himself in just in time to see the Neo-Sov ship launch the first of its missiles. "One away," he reported. "Two."

"One radar unit away as well," Boris replied. *"Dva. Tre."*

"Hang on a second," Raedawn said. "I'm going to brake a little so they get out ahead of us."

"Da, good idea. We are holding on."

Light thrust pushed them against their harnesses for a few seconds. "Okay, ditch the other three," David said.

"Adeen . . . dva . . . tre."

"Braking again."

"Go ahead."

This time she used the side thrusters as well, shoving them well away from their previous flight path.

The Neo-Soviet ship launched a whole flurry of missiles now that they saw what David's crew had just done. He counted six more launches. "We're two decoys shy," he said. "Let's hope the last ones home in on the first ones' explosions."

He waited, watching the tactical display as the missiles approached. The Neo-Soviet ship was firing its engines laterally now, either for the same reason that Raedawn had, or simply to make itself harder to hit.

"You going to shoot back, or just sit there?" Raedawn asked.

"Is there any point in wasting ammunition?" David said. "They won't be able to take another shot at us."

"We're at war," she reminded him. "When you're at

war, you kill as many of the enemy as you can. Even if they can't shoot at us again, we don't want to leave them alive to shoot at anyone else."

"Good point." David zeroed the crosshairs in on the on-coming ship and fired one of their three missiles.

"Hey!" yelled Boris. "That almost hit me!"

David tried to imagine the two spacesuited figures hanging on to handholds just outside the airlock. That would put the missile tubes right behind them, wouldn't it? "Sorry. Watch out for two more."

"We are ducking. Very low."

David centered the crosshairs on the oncoming ship and fired a second missile, then on a hunch he diverted his aim *behind* the enemy craft and fired his last shot.

"What the hell happened to that one?" Raedawn asked. It was clearly not headed in the right direction at all, and at this distance it would be another fifteen or twenty seconds before it locked on to the target. By then the Neo-Sov ship would have already passed it.

"Space is fast here," he explained. "The targeting computer corrects for the relative velocity it sees, but it doesn't know about conditions out there. Our missile is going to get there half a minute faster than the computer thinks it will."

She frowned. "Then so will theirs, won't they?"

"Right."

"So we shouldn't have slowed down, should we?"

"Yes, we should. We're going almost straight at them, so we want our decoys to hit the missiles before we do. They're running sideways to us, so we want to shoot behind them."

"That makes no sense," Raedawn said. "You always lead a target in motion."

"No," said Harxae over the radio. "He is correct. The

faster your projectile, the less you need to lead. Observe." An intense beam of near-ultraviolet light shot out from the flank of the ship, and a moment later one of the oncoming missiles burst into a fiery red cloud of plasma.

David and Raedawn exchanged a brief look of amazement. "He could've vaporized us at any time," she said softly.

Two more missiles zeroed in on the debris cloud and made an even bigger fireball. Four more exploded in a dotted line as they each hit a radar beacon.

"Where's that last one?" Raedawn asked nervously.

"I don't see it," David said. "The first couple of explosions must have thrown it off course enough to miss the beacons, so it's still coming. Trouble is, the tactical screen's tracking hundreds of pieces of debris now, and at least a dozen of them are heading straight for us. It could be any of them."

"Should I take evasive action?"

"No! If you use the jets, it'll home in on us for sure."

The violet light lanced out from the side of the ship twice more, but the targets it hit merely scintillated with reflections as fragments of metal vaporized.

"Come on, hit it," David muttered. The missile had to be nearly upon them by now.

"I'm trying," Harxae said, firing three more times, but he only hit more debris.

"I knew I should have stayed on Mars," Boris said.

In the upper left corner of the tactical display, the first two missiles David had fired swept past the Neo-Soviet ship, but the third one drew closer. The two dots merged, and a moment later space lit up with a huge flash as the explosion ripped the enemy to bits.

David shouted in triumph; but an instant later Harxae

fired one last time, and another brilliant fireball blossomed right in front of them. They barely had time to flinch before the ship rang with impacts. A big star-shaped crack blossomed in the front window.

"Aaaa!" someone screamed, but David couldn't tell if it was Boris or Harxae. Both of them were shouting at once as the ship rang with more impacts.

"Someone's hit," he said, unbuckling his harness and leaping out of the seat toward the back.

"Duh," said Raedawn, reaching for the emergency patch kit under her seat.

The outer airlock door slammed closed, and the air pressure in the ship dropped as the emergency spill valve flooded the lock with interior air instead of filling it from the storage tank. David yanked open the inner door and saw a mess of bright blue blood jetting out of Harxae's left thigh and filling the leg of his spacesuit. The alien was squeezing tight with his hands above the puncture, but he didn't seem to be doing much good. By the looks of it, whatever had hit him must have cut a major artery, and the Kalira apparently had blood pressure like a hydraulic line.

"Should we use a tourniquet?" he asked.

"*Blaxafi!*" the alien yelled. He tried to squeeze harder, but screamed again and fell back.

"Shit," David said. "Harxae, what do we do? Can I use a tourniquet on your leg?"

"Tranakit?"

"I don't think he can read our minds when he's in pain," Boris said.

"Doesn't look like it. Dammit we've got to do something." David yanked a cargo strap loose from the wall, praying that he was reading Harxae's intentions correctly. He wound it around the part of the leg he'd been squeezing, then made a double loop with the end of the strap and cinched it tight in one hard yank. The blood flow stopped.

Harxae screamed loud enough to hurt their ears even through his helmet. He jackknifed forward, clawing at his leg, but stopped when he saw what David had done. His arms quivered, but he clenched his fists and lay back. "*Naraxe*," he whispered.

"You're welcome." David glanced over at Boris. "Are you all right?"

"He was in front of me," Boris said softly. "He shielded me."

David measured the height of Harxae's leg against Boris's torso. "You're lucky. If you were standing side by side, the shot would have hit you in the gut."

"*Pravda*."

Out the front windows, Earth was a flat wall of blue and white. "Raedawn, how long till we get there?"

"Atmosphere in . . . maybe five minutes? Dirt in ten. Assuming we don't get shot at any more."

"Radio ahead and tell 'em we need a medical team waiting."

"Roger."

David looked at the green-gray alien stretched out before him, his skin more gray than green now. "And tell 'em to bring a veterinarian." A vet wouldn't know any more about Harxae's physiology than a doctor would, but maybe they would have more experience guessing how to treat unusual animals. And by the look of that bright blue blood, Harxae was going to be about as unusual inside as they came.

While Raedawn got on the radio, he and Boris carried Harxae into the cargo bay and helped him lean against the aft wall. They strapped him down this time, knowing it might be a rough trip if Raedawn had to take more evasive action. When Harxae was secure, Boris started to remove his spacesuit, but David shook his head and pointed forward at the cracked window. "Leave it on. We could blow out at any moment."

Boris swallowed hard and slipped one arm through another cargo strap, then with the other hand he reached for the emergency patch kit by the wall and began to repair the hole in the clear fabric over Harxae's leg.

"You want your suit?" David asked Raedawn.

"No time. Get up here. I need a navigator."

David looked at his own suit hanging in the airlock. It would take him only a minute to put it on.

"Now!" Raedawn screamed. "Shit!" The ship shuddered as she hit the attitude jets, throwing David against the bag containing Harxae's food. He pushed off from it toward the control room. A spacesuit wouldn't do him a bit of good if the ship didn't survive.

When he got into his chair, he could see what Raedawn was worried about. Low Earth orbit was filled with debris. It took him only a moment to realize where it had come from: one of the orbital battle stations had been totally destroyed. The tactical screen was full of blinking lights denoting the pieces' various probabilities of being weapons or targets. He zapped the display away with a swipe at the control panel and replaced it with the navigation grid. The same debris there, but this time with vector arrows showing their trajectories. Much more useful. Three lines blinked red where they crossed the ship's path.

"Left," he said. There was a gap there, but it only lasted a few seconds. "Up," he said, finding another gap. "Right. *Hard* right!"

He actually saw the piece of docking hatch flash past,

but it didn't hit them. A few seconds later something small did, putting another star in the window right in front of Raedawn.

She didn't flinch. She faced straight ahead, the control stick gripped in both hands and her eyes glued on the planet.

She had put a clear patch on the window in front of David while he was in back. He reached for the kit to patch this new crack, but she said, "Leave it! We don't have time for that."

He looked back to the nav screen. She was right. Another red line swept toward them. "Up!" he yelled.

She dodged. He called out another obstacle. She dodged again. Eventually they left the debris field behind and touched atmosphere.

"Now the fun starts," Raedawn muttered as flame began licking back from the nose of the ship.

13

T he shuttle had the shape of a watermelon seed with a bump on top. That bump was the control cabin, set a quarter of the way back to form a bubble like the cockpit of a jet fighter. It was supposed to be far enough back that a shock wave from the nose would direct oncoming air over the top, providing a cool pocket of safety for the pilot while the rest of the ship heated to incandescence.

Trouble was, the ship was entering the atmosphere at nearly double its normal speed, and the shock wave was much closer to the hull than usual. The top few centimeters of the control bubble were right in the flow of the ionized plasma, which hit it like a cutting torch.

David watched the high-temp glass begin to bubble on its outer surface. It was a hand's-width thick and designed to carry excess heat away by ablation, but there was a limit to how much of it could vaporize before its strength was compromised. Both panels were already cracked; if they shattered, the shards would slice off his and Raedawn's heads. Of course a millisecond later the pressure wave would slam through the shuttle and blow it to shreds, but somehow it was the threat of decapitation that made his breath come short and his heart pound.

"Angle us upward," he said. "Let the underside take the heat." The layer of foamed ceramic insulation that lined the bottom of the lifting body could withstand thousands of degrees more than the windows.

"If I do that, we'll skip off the atmosphere."

"Better that than burning up."

"If we skip, we'll come down again halfway around the planet." She didn't have to say anything more. That would put them directly over the Neo-Soviet heartland, and there was no way they could fight their way back to friendly territory from there.

They both stared at the shock wave streaming back from the shuttle's nose, trying to think of a third option. They were decelerating hard, their harnesses digging into their shoulders and hips, but not hard enough. The windows were already a third of the way gone, and the cracks were extending steadily outward.

"Can we at least shift from side to side a bit? Vary the angle of attack to spread out the heat a little?"

"Oh, sure. Yaw back and forth at mach thirty. Do you understand anything about dynamic instability?"

He did. They were riding a knife blade; the moment they tilted it the least bit out of true, it would start to flutter. Fighter jets flying at a tenth their speed could be ripped to pieces that way; there was no way the shuttle's airframe would withstand it. "Okay, dumb idea," he said. Desperation had a way of clouding logical thought.

The windows' outer surfaces were bubbling now like water on a stove. "We're going to burn through!" he shouted.

"Tell me something I don't know."

"Bank us upward!"

"We'll skip."

"I don't care! Bank us up." Even if they died at Neo-Soviet hands, they would have another few precious minutes of life first.

She nudged the nose upward, and the shuttle creaked ominously as the blast of air shifted from straight-on to slam into the underside. The windows quit bubbling, but the nose kept trying to pitch up even harder, and she had to struggle to keep it down. They were still going way too fast for flight. The shuttle behaved more like an arrow at this speed, but it didn't have enough fletching to make it dynamically stable. The center of pressure was way forward of the center of mass. If it tilted more than a few degrees, the weight of the engines in the back would flip the whole works end-for-end and send them screaming backward out of control.

David envisioned that just as clearly as the window failure, but in his mental picture, the flame was shooting the other way.

"Wait a sec," he said. "Let it go."

"Let what go?"

"Let us flip end-for-end."

She couldn't afford to look away from the flight controls, but he could see from her expression that she thought he'd gone totally insane. "Oh, that'd be smart. The back of the ship isn't designed to withstand any heat at all. We'd fry within seconds."

"Not if we fire the engines at full thrust. It's the Coanda effect. The drive flame will actually suck some of the oncoming air backward with it. We'll plow through our own exhaust, but it'll be coming at us a lot slower than what's hitting us now."

"This shuttle was never designed to descend under thrust."

"It wasn't designed to hit the atmosphere at mach thirty, either."

She dithered, clearly not trusting his crackpot idea, but she couldn't come up with anything better. In the end it was fate as much as volition that decided her; the shuttle pitched upward again and she tried to correct for it, but she hesitated a moment too long and lost her chance.

When David realized they were going over, he reached out and slapped the engine control, shoving the thrust all the way to full. For a moment the sudden acceleration matched the backward force from air friction, but the effect was only momentary. The ship pitched on around, roaring and shaking like a wounded dragon as it did.

Fortunately, it went over backward instead of forward; at least that way the shifting gee forces shoved them down into their seats instead of yanking them up against their harnesses. If that had happened, they would have broken their collarbones and shoulder blades and probably snapped their necks as well. As it was they only felt as if they were being crushed to death. Boris and Harxae weren't quite so lucky in back, having no acceleration chairs, but at least they were wedged deeper into their corner rather than thrown across the cargo hold.

The shuttle wound up upside down. That hardly mattered; heavy gees shoved them back in their chairs. David couldn't read the gee gauge to know for sure how much it was. His eyes were deformed from the thrust, blurring everything as if he were extremely farsighted. Neither he nor Raedawn could reach the controls to steer. All they could do was sit there, straining merely to breathe, while the ship plunged deeper and deeper into the atmosphere. They were totally at the mercy of gravity and aerodynamics now.

Boris was still wearing his spacesuit. His voice came over the intercom, laced with pain. "Are we dead yet?"

"Not . . . quite," David replied. "How's Harxae?"

"Holding on to me. If he hadn't, I would be up front with you. I lost grip on cargo strap when we first hit atmosphere."

David wondered what the Kalira was made of. Harxae looked too spindly to hold up his own weight, but if he was strong enough to hold the mass of a man against seven or eight gees after taking a flak wound in his leg, he was definitely made of sterner stuff than he appeared to be.

"What's your plan for landing?" Raedawn asked.

"I haven't thought that far ahead," he admitted.

Flames roared past the windows, but they were bright red barbecue flames, not the intense white-hot plasma they had been plowing through before. David tried to imagine what it must look like from the ground: a bright fireball streaking across the sky from horizon to horizon, like the Tunguska meteor, or the—

"Oh, shit."

"What?"

"What if they think we're an asteroid?"

She didn't need to reply. They both knew what would happen. The orbital battle platforms had been built mainly to defend against missile attacks, but they could fire upon meteors just as easily, vaporizing them before they hit the ground and causing just as much damage as a bomb.

"Tell them who we are!" Boris yelled.

Raedawn said, "Radio waves can't punch through all this ionized gas. We'll be blacked out for a couple more minutes."

"But they knew we were coming, right?" asked Boris.

"Sure they did, but they're expecting a ship, not a fireball."

Then David realized his mistake and started to laugh. It was more of a wheeze because of the elephant on his chest, but Boris and Raedawn understood it for what it was.

"What's so funny?" she asked.

"We're shooting flame out half a kilometer in *front* of us," he said. "They'll know we're a ship."

"Oh." She turned her head to the side and grinned weakly. "Duh."

"Of course if we're headed for inhabited land, they may blast us apart anyway. Nobody would believe we can set down gently coming in like this."

"We're over North Dakota headed for Montana," she said. "We're not endangering anybody but some cows."

"Oh. Good. So have you got any bright ideas on how to land this thing?"

The thrust gently eased while she thought it over. The more they decelerated, the less resistance the air provided. "We can't flip back around until we're moving a lot slower," she said, "but eventually we should drop to normal flight speed and then we should be able to do it. Hell, we could probably leave the engines running a few more seconds and already be in flight mode back the way we came without even having to turn around."

"Provided we don't hit ground first," Boris said. "What is altitude?"

David could see a little better now. He squinted at the gauge. "Sixteen kilometers. Forward velocity twenty-five hundred meters per second, dropping at three hundred meters per second." He tried to do the math in his head. "We've got . . . uh . . . fifty-three seconds until impact. Shit, that's not good. At—what are we doing, six gees? But that's dropping. At say five gees average, that'll take us . . . fifty seconds to come to rest. Jesus, that's going to be tight. Raedawn, can we curve our flight path any?"

"Not yet."

"How 'bout—"

"Once we get down below a hundred kicks per second or so. Not before."

"But that's only . . . four or five seconds from impact!"

"Do *you* want to try flying this thing backward at high velocity?"

"No." She was a much better pilot than he. If she couldn't do it, it couldn't be done.

Fortunately, they weren't picking up any more downward velocity. That seemed to be nearly constant, though if they hit at that speed they'd still leave nothing but a crater. They would have to thrust straight down at full power for at least six seconds to cancel that motion, which left them no time at all to turn around and land like they were supposed to. The agravs could absorb a little velocity, but the effect would be minuscule until the very last moment.

"Brace yourselves for impact," he said. "We're going to have to land backward."

"Could we at least not do it upside down?" said Boris.

"Picky, picky, picky," Raedawn said. She reached out through the decreasing gee force and used the rotational thrusters to bring them around, then with a what-the-hell shrug she fired the bottom-side jets on both sides. They were only good for a few meters per second of thrust, but at this point every spare meter counted.

"Impact in twenty," she said.

"Landing," David said. "Think of it as 'landing.' "

"I'd think of it as a snowflake falling on a cotton ball if I thought it would make any difference," she said. "Fifteen."

"Please, no countdown," said Boris. "I would rather be surprised."

"Chicken."

Raedawn reached forward again, straining to keep her hands in place over the controls.

David looked out the windows. It was hard to see clearly through the melted glass near the top, but the section closest to the bottom was still optically flat. The horizon was visible through the flames rushing around from behind the ship: jagged mountains to one side and green fields out the other. A double line of highway snaked through the fields. That would be I-90. He had driven that road once on the way from Seattle to Yellowstone Park, in an old hovercraft that needed to follow its gentle inclines through the mountains.

"Call 'em out," Raedawn said.

He looked back at the controls. Right. The pilot should look outside; the navigator should read the indicators. "Forward velocity four-sixty," he said. "Down two-eighty." The forward velocity was steadily dropping at five gees, fifty meters per second per second, but the vertical was only dropping in the single digits. "Forward three-seventy. Three-twenty. Two-eighty. Down two-seventy."

He kept calling out the figures, and as he did, he saw Raedawn tweak the attitude jets ever so slightly. The direction of *down* changed subtly, and now the vertical rate was changing almost as fast as the horizontal. The shuttle wobbled once and she cursed, but she got it under control again a second later.

"Forward one hundred!" he yelled when the magic number clicked past. "Down one-twenty." Now they were dropping faster than they were moving sideways.

He risked a glance out the window, but wished he hadn't. The mountains were way above them now, and it looked like the ship was about to smack into the ground at any moment.

Raedawn switched on the agravs. That shot her control all to hell again, but it didn't matter anymore. The ship shed the last of its horizontal velocity, and the mass-repelling effect shoved upward harder and harder the closer they came to the ground, building up to a spine-numbing ten gees before they ran out of room.

The rear landing legs hit first, then the front, slamming hard into the dirt. Raedawn killed the engines and the agravs just as the ship began to pitch over. It teetered on the front legs for a second, almost going over onto its top, but it finally settled back down on its legs.

In the sudden silence, David said, "Nice landing."

She snorted. "Thanks for calling out those crucial last few meters."

"Anytime," he said before he realized she was being sarcastic.

She ignored him. "Look," she said, pointing. "Here comes the welcoming committee."

He followed her outstretched finger. Sure enough, off in the distance, roaring straight toward them through what looked like a million hectares of wheat, was a single vehicle no doubt bearing a very irate farmer.

14

I t took all David's courage to open both airlock doors and step outside without a spacesuit on. He knew he was on Earth, but he'd been conditioned by years of living in space stations and on Mars. There, death waited beyond the airlock unless you protected yourself against vacuum and cold, and he had to consciously remind himself that here there was air and that the temperature was shirtsleeve comfortable.

The sky held puffy white clouds suspended in a vast expanse of blue, but the sun was not the same as he remembered it. Instead of a small disk too bright to look at, the swirling nebula that Harxae called the "Tkona" filled a couple hands' width of sky. It shone less intensely, and there were half a dozen black specks from other planets between it and Earth, but it made up for that in size. He wondered if it provided the right wavelengths for plants, and if the total incoming radiation would keep the atmosphere warm enough through the winter.

If there *was* a winter. Earth's axis could tilt in an entirely new direction here. And if that was the case, then the planet's normal convection patterns could break down, isolating air masses into bands like on Jupiter, or engulfing the entire globe in storms like the ones that periodically swept around Mars. He knelt down to look at the wheat stalks. They were charred black right near the ship, but they were green just a few meters away. They looked a bit withered on top even farther out, but it was hard to tell if that was from drought or from the shuttle's fiery landing. Either way, it was a good thing they hadn't come down a month later. If the grain had been ready to harvest, they could have set half the state on fire.

It was harder than he thought to stand up again. He was going to have to be careful until he adjusted to Earth's gravity. Fortunately Raedawn had come out just behind him, and she reached out to steady him when he wavered.

"Thanks," he said.

She nodded back inside. "Harxae's in pretty bad shape. Boris doesn't look too good, either. I radioed for help, but it'll be a while. We're a long ways from where we were supposed to set down."

"There must be a hospital somewhere around here."

"Sure doesn't look like it."

"We'll find out in a minute," he said. The pickup bounced over an irrigation ditch and roared the final few hundred meters toward them, its oversized rubber tires leaving wide tracks in the wheat.

"You'd think he'd use agrav in a wheat field," David observed, but then he realized the truck didn't *have* agrav. It looked like it had been built in the previous century, and when it drew close enough to see the rusted body panels he realized that it had probably been built near the beginning of that century. He half expected it to have an internal combustion engine, but it did at least have an electric motor.

The driver brought it to a skidding stop just a few steps

away from the airlock. The door screeched with a metal-on-metal grate that set David's teeth on edge, but he held his smile for the farmer, who was scowling as he looked over the scorched shuttle and the two passengers standing before him. He wore a green and brown cap with "Bob's Steak Out" stitched above the bill. The cap shaded a fiftyish face that had seen a lot of sun in its life but no razor in the last week or so. David had expected a flannel shirt and bib overalls to go with the truck, but this guy wore a green-and-gray-striped T-shirt and blue jeans instead.

"Well, what's your story?" the man finally asked.

"I'm Captain David Hutchins, Union Space Command. This is Raedawn Corona, of the same. We're here from Mars to see what we can do to put Earth back where it belongs."

The farmer slowly nodded. "Howard Robertson, and that'd be fine with me. Doesn't look like you're in much shape to be moving planets around anytime soon, though. What happened? Get a bee in your shirt on final approach?"

Raedawn, caught unaware by the image, burst out laughing. "Ha! No, but we sure as hell got stung. We had to take out a few ships and dodge what's left of a battle station on our way in."

"That'd be Liberty Station." Howard scratched the back of his head with a dirty finger. "One o' the Miller boys helped build that. He wasn't happy to hear it'd got hit."

He ought to be happy he wasn't on it at the time, David thought, but he prudently kept his mouth shut.

Raedawn wasn't so courteous. "About five hundred laser jocks aren't happy, either," she said. "I just hope they fried some Soviet bacon before they got hit."

"Yeah," said Howard dubiously. He either didn't know or wasn't saying.

David wondered if he and Raedawn knew more about

the situation on Earth than the locals did. "What all's happened here since you went through the spatial anomaly?"

The farmer squinted at him for a moment. Then he angled his head toward the mountains that rose like jagged teeth only a few kilometers away. "I'm not sure about all that, but we got plenty goin' on around here. We got us a new mountain range, for one thing."

"What?" David looked up at the majestic peaks. Had the transition been violent enough to raise an entire new range? The earthquakes must have been incredible. But the smooth wheat field didn't look like it had felt a tremor. Just to be sure he'd heard the farmer right, he asked, "Those mountains weren't here before?"

"Do they look like the Bitterroots?"

"I wouldn't know."

"Well, I would, and they don't. They're somethin' else entirely; grew up out o' the ground like a ring o' mushrooms. Dammed up the Clark's Fork tighter'n a bung in a barrel. Gonna play hell with irrigation." He sighed and looked back at his wheat field. "Not like it's gonna matter much. Damn weird weather's already messed up the crops, and now you come in here and burn half an acre on top of it. I tell you, it just ain't been my week."

"Week?" asked David. "Earth's only been gone a day."

The farmer looked at him askance. "Maybe a Martian day, but it's been seven here."

David groaned. "Shit. Temporal effects, too. That's going to complicate things even more."

Raedawn said, "You don't really think you're going to be able to send Earth back through the rabbit hole, do you? After seeing all these other planets stuck here, and after what Harxae told us?"

David felt a tightness in his chest at the thought of how

far they were from home. "I don't know," he said, "but I'm not going to give up without even trying."

A voice from inside the shuttle said, "Stop chitchat and get help!"

There was no disguising that accent. Howard squinted to see through the airlock into the dark interior and said, "You got a prisoner in there?"

David hesitated. What was Boris's status, anyway? Technically he was a political refugee, but that probably wouldn't make any points with the farmer. Nor would it impress the Union military. But David wouldn't let him be treated like a prisoner, either, not after all he'd done.

He took a deep breath and said, "He's part of the crew. We're all members of the New Mars Alliance. The Union and the Neo-Soviet forces on Mars patched up our differences in order to mount a rescue mission." He locked eyes with Raedawn, defying her to say otherwise.

Howard was skeptical enough without her help. "The Russkies made peace? On Mars? Next you'll be sayin' you've got Martians to help you out, too."

David grinned. "Well, as a matter of fact . . ." He held out his hand, inviting Howard to have a better look inside.

The farmer stepped into the airlock, then did a wonderfully theatrical double-take when his eyes adjusted enough to see who waited in the cargo hold. "Jesus Mary," he said. "You weren't shittin', were you? What happened to its leg?"

"He got hit by some space debris."

Howard backed away and continued to gape at Harxae with his mouth hanging open. Then his mouth snapped shut as a thought occurred to him. He took a step closer. "You been releasin' that tourniquet every once in a while?"

"What?"

"You can't just tie off a leg and 'spect it to live,"

Howard said. "You gotta let some blood into it from time to time or you might as well just chop it off."

"Oh. Excuse me." David squeezed past him and bent down next to Harxae's leg. It was pasty gray, rather than the greenish color it had been. "This is probably going to hurt," David said as he took the tourniquet in his hands.

Harxae said, *"Fanorxa,"* and squeezed his eyes shut. Apparently he was still in too much pain for telepathy.

David loosened the knot. Harxae winced, but didn't cry out, even when blood started squirting into the leg of his clear spacesuit again.

"Blue, eh?" Howard said with more bravado than the shaky tone of his voice would suggest. "Guess that makes sense. We live on a blue planet and have red blood, so it stands to reason Martians would—"

"He's not actually a Martian," David said. "He's a Kalira. From one of the planets up there." He pointed upward.

Even though they were in the cargo hold, Howard got the idea. "Oh. Well, he ain't from around here, that's for sure. That'll probably do."

David cinched the tourniquet down again and tied it off. Harxae let out a ragged breath and slumped back against Boris, who winced in pain but said nothing.

"How you doing?" David asked him. "Where does it hurt?"

"Everywhere," Boris said. "I think I break ribs, maybe hip. I also bit tongue."

Howard chuckled softly. "Insult to injury. Well, welcome to the U.S. of A. We'll patch you back up good as new in no time."

David didn't think it would be wise to remind him that the U.S. of A. was no longer a nation. It was just part of the

North American Union now. Apparently Boris didn't think it wise to point that out, either. He just nodded weakly and said, "*Spa*—thank you."

"How close is the nearest hospital?" David asked.

"Missoula," said the farmer. "'Bout fifty miles."

David had to make the conversion to kilometers in his head. Either way, it was half an hour in a hovercar, but they didn't have a hovercar.

"Will that truck of yours make it that far?"

"Prob'ly. I'll have to stop and recharge 'fore we go." He frowned, and added, "It'll be a bumpy ride."

"Let's check on the cavalry first," Raedawn said. She stepped past them into the control cabin and keyed the transmitter. "Union Command, Union Command, come in Union Command. This is Mars vessel *Shadow One*."

"Come in, *Shadow One*."

"What's your E.T.A.? We've got two wounded, and we're forty-five minutes or so from the nearest hospital."

"We'll be there in fifteen. Hold tight."

"Roger."

She leaned back into the cargo hold. "You heard?"

"Yeah."

Howard didn't look happy. "What's the matter?" David asked him.

Howard walked over to the airlock's outer door and looked out, silhouetted against the bright green wheat field and the mountains beyond. "I imagine they'll crush another acre when they land."

He was probably right. "I imagine the government will pay you for the damage," David said.

"Ain't worth the paperwork," Howard replied. He sighed, then looked back in at the three Martians and the Kalira. "What the hell. Think of it as my contribution to the cause. If you can actually put us back where we belong, I'll give you the whole harvest. But see if you can't manage to leave those damned mountains behind."

"I'll see what I can do," David said, eyeing them dubiously through the airlock. To someone who planned to move a planet, moving mountains should be a piece of cake. If he told himself that often enough, he might even start to believe it.

15

Their ambulance turned out to be a sky-blue troop carrier. Its camouflage was so good and its agrav approach so silent that they barely realized it was there before the vehicle settled down beside their shuttle and the door rolled up into the hull. Two soldiers in khaki stepped out, carrying a stretcher.

"Where's the wounded?" the first one asked. She was a big, round-faced woman with hair even shorter than Raedawn's and an equally no-nonsense expression.

The other soldier was a young man, barely in his twenties, who couldn't have weighed sixty kilos. David wondered how he could lift his half of the stretcher when it was empty, much less occupied, but he trotted along behind the woman without apparent effort.

They entered the ship and stopped dead at the sight of Harxae. The woman was better at hiding her shock than the young man was. He began to shake. She turned to him and said sharply, "We'll take the human first." He struggled to pull himself together as they helped Boris onto the stretcher.

The two of them carried Boris across to their ship, then came back for Harxae.

The stretcher was too short for the Kalira. "Could you scrunch up a little?" the woman asked him, not waiting to see if he understood before she took him by the shoulders and scooted him upward so his head was right at the top of the webbing. He cried out when they taped his legs to the handles so his feet wouldn't drag on the ground, but he let them do it, and a moment later they lifted him up and carried him away.

David and Raedawn had gotten their travel bags out of the pile of webbing. They carried those across to the other ship, along with Harxae's food. His talisman had been lost in space when he was hit, and their own weapons they left on board, along with the scientific instruments. They could retrieve those later.

"We'll get this ship out of your field as soon as we can," he told Howard, offering his hand to shake.

The farmer had a strong grip. "Take your time," he said. "I ain't doin' nothin' with this part of it 'til the grain ripens anyway."

Raedawn closed the airlock, and David noticed that she palmed the security plate as she did. So did Howard, but if he was offended, he didn't show it. "I'll keep an eye on 'er for you, missy," he said. "Won't nobody mess with it while I'm around."

"Thanks," she said.

"Let's go," said the lady medic.

They climbed inside the vehicle, David and Raedawn holding on to the walls for support in the high gravity. Boris and Harxae were side by side on exam tables; the woman began cutting off the leg of Harxae's spacesuit and the man did the same for Boris's entire suit.

"Can we help?" David asked.

"Nope," said the woman. "Just grab a seat and hang on. We've got it under control."

There was a bench running along both side walls. Raedawn and David settled gratefully onto the end of the one closest to the door and pulled the flight harnesses down to buckle themselves in against turbulence. They felt a moment of extra weight as the pilot—hidden behind a closed door—lifted off and angled them forward under heavy acceleration, then it eased off and the ride steadied out. There were no windows, so they couldn't see where they were going, but David remembered a name.

"Grand Falls?" he asked.

"Great Falls," the woman replied. "Space Force base there. General Lamott wants to talk to you."

The name rang a faint bell. David knew a Lamott once, back in college. The idea of Perry working his way up the military structure quickly enough to be in command of a Space Force base seemed ludicrous, but he supposed Perry might think the same thing about David's assignment to the secret Mars mission.

"Did you say 'Lamott' or 'Lamont'?" he asked.

"Lamott."

How many Lamotts could there be? It wasn't that common a name. "Perry Lamott?"

"Yep." She loosened the tourniquet on Harxae's leg, then immediately tightened it again when blue blood squirted straight up to the ceiling.

David winced, but the woman hardly batted an eye, so he asked, "Short guy? Red hair if he's not bald by now? Goofy grin?"

"I've never seen him smile, but the rest of the description matches."

The other medic said, "That's him. He grins a *lot* when

he's out on maneuvers. He likes to be up front where the action is."

"That'd be him," David said. "He always loved things that make a big bang. He and I blew up a physics lab once."

Raedawn leaned back against the hull. "Wonderful. Two nutcases in the same room. You want to drop me off somewhere along the way?"

Neither medic replied to that. The one working on Harxae cleaned off the skin around his wound and pressed a gauze pad against it, then tried loosening the tourniquet again. She had to push with both hands to keep the blood from seeping out, but Harxae's leg regained its normal greenish color. His breathing quickened as he fought to keep from screaming.

"I wish I could give you something for the pain," she said, "but I have no idea what would work or what would kill you." She looked up at David and Raedawn for a second. "What can you tell me about him?"

"His name's Harxae," David said. "He calls his race the Kalirae, and says they've been stuck here for over two and a half centuries. We met him and a companion just after we came through from the solar system, but . . . uh . . . their ship was damaged, and Gavwin was killed in the spatial anomaly that brought us here. So we decided to bring Harxae home with us, and we had a little run-in with the Neo-Sov welcoming committee, and here we are."

Raedawn nudged his net bag with her right foot. "We brought his food, which might give you a clue to his body chemistry, but he'll probably be able to tell you himself when he calms down. He's telepathic."

The medics exchanged glances, clearly wondering if Raedawn needed medical help as well.

"It's true," David said. "And yes, that might pose a security risk. You should probably call ahead and make sure nobody with sensitive information in their heads hangs around the hospital while he's there."

He could tell they didn't believe him, either, but the cover-your-ass instinct was strong in the military. Now the medics had someone to blame it on when the people at the base told them they were nuts. So the male medic took a moment to knock on the control cabin door and relay the information, then he went back to work on Boris.

They were met at the spaceport by a phalanx of soldiers in full body armor, carrying ridiculously large assault rifles, flamethrowers, and short-range rocket launchers. They wore full coverage helmets with their visors sealed down tight, as if that could deflect the Kalira's psychic ability. They stood ready to fire as two more medics entered the transport and helped carry the patients out on stretchers.

It was all David could do to keep from laughing at the sight of the Union army ready to annihilate a busted-up ex-Russian spy and a flak-wounded alien. As he hobbled down the ramp, he whispered to Raedawn, "Where were these guys when we needed 'em, eh?"

She snorted and whispered back, "Playing with their toys, no doubt."

They were the only ones amused by the sight. Half a dozen grim-faced MPs surrounded the two of them and led them off toward a waiting hovercar, while Boris and Harxae were carried in the opposite direction to an ambulance.

"I'd like to go with them," David said.

"They'll be taken care of," said one of the MPs.

David was sure they would, but this excessive show of force made him wonder just what "taken care of" meant to these people. He couldn't imagine them being stupid enough to kill their patients just for being foreigners, but it sure didn't look like they planned to treat them well, either.

"They're friends of mine," he said. "And as soon as the general finds out who they are, they're going to be friends of his, too, so be sure to treat them right."

"They'll be taken care of," the MP said again.

There was no use arguing. David and Raedawn climbed into the car and rode with two of the MPs in the seat across from them as a third drove them down a tree-lined grass hoverpath through the base.

The buildings they passed showed evidence of earthquake damage: broken windows, cracked walls, and the like. One had collapsed entirely.

"What was the transition like?" David asked.

The same MP—he was apparently the designated speaker for the group—said, "The Change? It was . . . strange."

"Strange how?"

"Dark. There was lightning all over the place. We had earthquakes, weird noises, wind; you name it. Kalispell got a rain of frogs, only the frogs had three eyes and spit acid. Half the trees in the Bob Marshall Wilderness turned to crystal. Stuff like that."

"We saw the mountains that rose up near where we crashed."

"That, too. We took rock samples, and they're not terrestrial. Not Lunar, either."

"I'd like to see the specimens," David said.

"You'll have to talk to the general about that." The MP cleared his throat, then said, "What did it look like from Mars?"

David told him about the black cloud and the lightning-filled tendrils of darkness. Raedawn added her observations as well. When David described his experiments with the fusion generator in the lab, the MP said, "You left it on after you saw what it was doing? Sounds like you got more balls than brains."

David felt a moment's anger, but he let it go. People never seemed to understand his determination to discover how the universe worked. Nor his desire to find a place where he could live in peace while he did it. "Maybe so," he said, "but what I learned just may help get Earth back where it belongs."

The MP shook his head. "I don't know if I want to go through that again."

"Talk to the alien we brought with us. If what he says is true, we really don't want to stick around here."

The car slipped into a parking spot near a four-story brick office building. More MPs waited there to escort David and Raedawn inside, where they were taken up to the top floor and whisked straight into an office that looked more like a corporate president's than a military general's. Their feet sank into thick carpeting as they crossed the outer office, soft music played through recessed speakers in the ceiling, and overstuffed couches waited for them to sit in.

The adjutant at the reception desk—looking no more military than the office in her form-fitting blue dress uniform—waved them toward an inner office, saying, "He's expecting you."

They passed through the mahogany double doors into an office big enough to have an echo if it hadn't been filled with more soft furniture and models of spacecraft and paintings on the walls. A massive mahogany desk stood at the far end of the room, set sideways so a person sitting there could look out the window without having his back to the door. The desk chair was turned toward the window, and the top of someone's head was just visible over the back of the large chair. The view overlooked a grassy parade ground, empty at the moment save for a flock of blackbirds pecking around for food.

From here it seemed as if nothing was wrong with the world. There was no sign of environmental disaster, no sign that the Union and the Neo-Soviet empire were at war, nor that the Earth had joined a maelstrom of other captured planets slowly spiraling into a planet-eating maw of destruction.

"Hello?" said David. Their escort had stopped at the door, letting him and Raedawn go ahead.

"By God, it is you!" said a familiar voice as the chair wheeled around. The man stood and David saw the familiar face that went with the voice: Perry Lamott had bulked out a little in the chest and let his hair grow, but otherwise he hadn't changed much since their college days.

"It's me," David said. "And this is Raedawn Corona. She's our intelligence officer. Good pilot, too."

"Pleased," said Lamott.

"Likewise," said Raedawn. They looked at one another for a few seconds, sizing each other up in a way that made David feel like he wasn't even in the room.

"So how'd you wind up here?" David asked.

Lamott glanced over at him, then back at Raedawn. "You mean as opposed to a lab somewhere?" He shrugged. "I got drafted. Decided I didn't want to be cannon fodder, so I went into R and D and took officer candidate school on the side. Got lucky a couple of times and got promoted to a desk, and then found out I was actually pretty good at telling people what to do. Who'da thunk, eh?"

"You always were good at getting other people into trouble."

"True. It's a gift. So how'd *you* get here? I imagine your story is a little more exciting."

David shrugged. "Oh, just the usual harrowing trip through a rift in space into an alternate dimension. No big deal."

Raedawn didn't look like she thought it was so funny, and asked permission to use the facilities.

"Through there," Perry said, pointing to a door that stood ajar behind the desk.

She walked across the office and slipped through the door.

Lamott watched her until she closed the door behind her. Then he held out his hand to David, and the two shook hands. "It's been a long time, Dave. If anybody can figure out how to put us back where we belong, you're the guy."

"Maybe," said David. "I've got a couple of ideas, but even if they work, it's not going to be easy."

"What sort of ideas?" Perry asked.

"Electromagnetic pulse bombs. Thousands of EMP bombs all over the planet, and thousands of plasma bombs in space just ahead of it in orbit. If we can stretch what's left of the anomaly close enough when we blow the EMP bombs, it should swallow the planet just like it did before, and then when we're in it good and deep, the plasma bombs will blow the anomaly apart. When the Kalirae missile did that to the little one we came through, we could see stars for a second where it was. I think the middle of it went back into normal space."

"Kalirac missile?" asked Perry. "I thought these aliens were supposed to be friendly."

"It's a complicated story," David said. "According to them, they're about as friendly as anybody here, but that's a relative term."

Perry walked over to a cabinet next to the couch and opened it to reveal a well-stocked bar. "Drink?" he asked.

David hadn't realized how tense he was until he felt it sliding away. The world was still in peril, but for a moment he had found an island of calm amid the craziness. For a moment he could relax and let someone else be responsible for holding things together.

He settled into the couch, grateful for its support in Earth's heavy gravity. "Make mine a double," he said.

16

They were already deep in discussion of the anomaly and David's theories for how to go back through it when Raedawn rejoined them.

"Vodka tonic," she said before Lamott could ask.

"Not many people drink vodka these days," he said, nonetheless finding a bottle of Stolichnaya in his cabinet and mixing her drink with a generous jigger.

"More for me," she said. "Besides, it's part of our new alliance on Mars. We drink vodka, they drink beer."

"New alliance?" Lamott waited for her to sit down. When she took the other end of the same couch where David was seated, Lamott changed seats to sit in a recliner across from her instead of David. He had to turn his head sideways to say to David, "You didn't tell me the Union had formed an alliance with the Neo-Soviets on Mars."

David nearly choked on his scotch. He had used that cover story on the farmer, but he hadn't planned to lie to the military. Especially not to a former friend who could probably see through him in a second.

Raedawn had no such worry. "There's nothing like watching your home planet vanish to make you feel alone in the universe. Neither side had the stomach for fighting afterward." She glanced over at David.

Lamott was still looking at her. "I hope the truce is stable."

"Very," Raedawn said, not missing a beat.

"Good. We'll need that if we're going to convince the Neo-Sovs here."

Raedawn lost her cool for a moment. "Convince the Neo-Sovs?" she echoed.

"David's been explaining his idea for placing EMP bombs around the planet and blowing them all at once to attract the anomaly again."

She looked at David, then at Lamott, as if they were both completely insane.

Lamott seemed not to notice. "It just might work, but we can't do it without everyone's cooperation." To David he said, "This is all assuming you can get us some proof of concept, of course. Our own people won't go for it without that, much less the Sovs. Nobody will go for it unless we can send something else back home first."

David grimaced. "They'll have to, because we're only going to get one shot at this. The process involves destroying the anomaly, and there's only one of them now. We can probably show proof of concept for drawing it toward the Earth again by detonating a few EMPs in a line between it and here. In fact we probably ought to do that just to make sure it doesn't close up again before we're ready to go, but as far as the actual transition goes, they'll just have to take my word for it."

Perry tapped the side of his glass with a fingernail. It made a soft *ding, ding, ding* while he thought, and went silent when he spoke. "Look, David, you know as well as I do that no one's going to be willing to take a risk like that without proof that it could actually work. Not to mention that the Neo-Sovs will probably think it's a ruse to get them to lower their guard."

David thought without tapping. "We've got the star pattern we saw through the explosion when Gavwin accidentally touched off the Kalirae missile. If that's recognizable, it's proof that we opened a hole back into the solar system. Then there's the light spectrum from the anomaly itself. If it's sunlight coming through from the other side, then the spectrum ought to match the Sun's. That should prove there's still a connection to the other side."

"That's something, but it might not be enough."

"It'll have to be. We don't want to blow up our only escape route in a test shot."

Raedawn looked incredulous. "Plenty of people aren't going to want all those bombs going off around the planet for a live shot, either. They're *weapons,* remember? Designed to wipe out unshielded electronics. You're going to fry every computer and microwave and idiot box in the world."

"People can build Faraday cages around their electronics," David said.

"Most people can't even spell 'Faraday,'" Raedawn countered. "Anyway, why do we need to put them in Soviet territory in the first place? Why not just on our side of the planet?"

David said, "Because we don't know the anomaly will envelop the whole Earth a second time. Shoving only half of it back into normal space might be kind of a Pyrrhic victory."

The three of them sat for a few seconds, thinking it over. Perry's soft tapping joined the rattle of ice cubes as the other two sipped their drinks, then he said, "You sure we can't create another anomaly when we need it? You were able to do it once."

"From the other side," David said. "The missiles we shot at the Kalirae and at the Neo-Sov ship had plenty of magnetic pulse in them, and they didn't open anything up. You can stretch an anomaly around from this side once they're formed, but I think creating them has to happen from normal space." He took another swallow of scotch, then added, "Besides that, I have no idea how to direct where an anomaly goes even if I could open one up. This universe is obviously a lot smaller than ours; if we punch a separate hole into normal space a kilometer away from the old one, who's to say it would even be in our own solar system on the other side? It might be somewhere in the Andromeda galaxy."

Lamott was silent for a moment, nodding to himself. "For now, the next step is to see what else can be learned from this Kalira of yours. If it's true what he says about a constant state of warfare in this place, I don't think it would be a good idea for me to be present."

"Harxae," said Raedawn, setting her glass down on the end table beside the couch. "We should go see how he is."

Lamott shook his head. "Not yet, Captain. What else do you know about his telepathic ability?"

"Not much, other than that he's got it."

David said, "I suspect he was using it from ship to ship while he and Gavwin were learning our language. That was a distance of maybe two hundred meters, but there were no other minds around to confuse things. I don't know how much range he's got. We'll have to ask."

"And we'll have to test his answers. In the meantime, I'd better stay away."

"Right." David hesitated, then said, "We do know that

pain keeps him from reading minds, even when he wants to."

"Let's hope we don't have to act on that knowledge, but it's useful to know he can be shut down without killing him." Lamott stood up. "All right, go ahead and check on him. He's going to want to see a friendly face. In the meantime, I'll get on the horn with the Pentagon and bring them up to speed on the situation here. We're going to have to convince a few people your theory holds water, but if you've got the data you claim you do, I think it'll be possible."

"We should bring the shuttle here before something happens to it," David said, also standing.

"Already happening." Lamott offered his hand to Raedawn. "Good landing, by the way. Anytime you want to apply for a pilot position under my command, you've got it."

"Thanks," she said, accepting his hand and rising to her feet. She gave him a slight smile, not enough to be encouraging but not enough to shut him down, either. David found himself wishing she would be less mysterious for once and just tell the guy to bug off, but he supposed it was none of his business.

The hovercar took them back across the base to the hospital, where they found both Boris and Harxae in an intensive-care room with two guards—still in full battle armor—at the door. The room's interior, at least, was more friendly. Its only windows overlooked the nurses' station, but it was brightly lit and had a huge entertainment screen on the wall. At the moment the screen was displaying a forest scene, either recorded or one of the live feeds from Yellowstone Park that had become so popular in recent years.

Boris, encased in an ultrasonic tissue regenerator from

waist to neck, looked a little like a barrel-chested robot stranded on his back. Harxae lay stretched across two beds set end to end on one side of the room. His color had returned, even in the injured leg, which bore an oval patch anchored down with high-strength filament tape.

"How you guys doing?" David asked.

Boris rapped on the metal case around his chest, careful not to hit any of the controls or blinking red indicator lights. "Three broken ribs and dislocated hip, but good as new in week, they tell me."

"Good. Harxae? Can you understand us again?"

The alien nodded his long head. "Yes. I brought my own medication. My thanks for the rescue."

"Yeah, but I don't think we'd have made it if you hadn't flamed those missiles. That talisman of yours is a neat little gadget."

"Was," said Harxae. "I let go of it when I was hit."

"Hopefully you won't need it anymore anyway. The commander here is an old friend of mine, and he thinks our plan to shove Earth back through the anomaly could be worth the risk. He's trying to get approval right now. With any luck, we'll be out of the fighting from now on."

Harxae made the lip-smacking sound that Kalirae used for laughter. "With any luck we wouldn't be here."

17

Harxae claimed a telepathic range of less than a hundred meters when there were other minds about. Trouble was, nobody could figure out a good way to test that statement. They could disprove it if he was ever found with information he couldn't have gotten from someone closer by, but they couldn't think of a test that would produce positive proof of a negative condition. After all, as David was fond of saying, absence of evidence was not evidence of absence.

Lamott therefore declined to meet the Kalira until such a test could be found. He called to extend his best wishes, covering up the camera on his end so Harxae couldn't get a mental image of him to help focus on, but Harxae claimed he could barely understand him without the telepathic link to give his words meaning. He gleaned enough information from David and Raedawn to answer, but it was like looking up every word in a bilingual dictionary. His response was fluent, which David thought was proof that he was scamming them, but Harxae picked up on his thought and said, "I'm addressing him with thoughts I find in your mind. If I had to make up everything from scratch, I would be just as slow at that as I am at translating what he says to me."

David tried to think of a way to test that, but even if Harxae could read his mind halfway around the planet, the alien could always hold back when not in the same room and it would look like he couldn't.

Lamott assured the alien that his caution wasn't personal, and that as soon as they could confirm Harxae's abilities and intentions, he would be glad to meet him. They left it at that, but David had barely disconnected when Harxae suddenly sat straight up in bed and said, "We are in danger."

"What?" asked David. "From whom?"

"Someone is approaching the building with the intent to kill us all."

David instinctively looked toward the window, but it only faced the nurse station. The two on duty were busy entering patient data into the computer system and answering the phone, oblivious to any danger. He could see one of the guards beside the door, too, but the soldier merely stood at parade rest watching the interior of the room, not looking for trouble from outside.

"Are you sure?" David asked.

"Positive. His name is Rick Stockwell. A sergeant, serial number 32956583. He was instructed by General Lamott himself to assassinate all four of us because we pose a security risk to the Union. He is carrying a 'pitbull' assault rifle with exploding bullets in a hundred-round magazine. He also has a 'pug' hand pistol with exploding rounds and two fragmentation grenades. He dislikes the thought of committing murder and actually hopes to die in the assault rather than live with the moral repercussions of it, but he will obey his orders. He has just entered the elevator."

"Shit!" David said. "The son of a bitch was just stringing us along until he could get us all together. And he called to make sure, but he didn't have the stomach to listen to us die."

Raedawn bent down as if to hide behind Boris's bed, and Boris started poking frantically at buttons on his regenerator, trying to find the one that would release him from its confinement, but David grabbed the door and yanked it open. "We're under attack!" he said to the guards. "Somebody heard there was a Neo-Sov here. He's in the elevator right now!"

"How do you know that?" one of them asked.

"The alien's telepathic, remember?"

Just then the elevator door opened, and an armored soldier stepped out.

"Halt!" cried the guard David had been talking to. Both of them leveled their weapons at the newcomer.

The armored soldier halted, then slowly raised his helmet visor and said, "Sergeant Stockwell here to replace whichever one of you wants to take a break. By the sound of it, maybe that ought to be both of you."

"We . . . uh . . . we haven't gotten any orders to take a break."

"That's because I'm bringin' 'em. Here." Stockwell reached beneath his armored vest.

"Slowly," said the first guard.

David heard Raedawn come up beside him. In her hand was a slim tube with wires running from it to the heel of her shoe. He recognized it immediately: a pulse laser, and the heel was the battery. It would be good for maybe ten shots before the tube melted, but unless that battery had more zap than it looked like, there was no way she could punch through battle armor with it.

He moved aside to give her room anyway. Harxae came

up beside him to stand next to the window in full view of the assassin.

The assassin pulled a piece of paper from his vest pocket and unfolded it. He stepped closer to hand it to the door guards, but then stopped suddenly, saying, "Yes, sir" into his headset. Just then the nurse who had been talking on the phone swung the arm-mounted screen out to the new arrival. David glimpsed Lamott's face on the flat screen as it swung around.

"Sergeant Stockwell," said Lamott. "You are to stand down. Do you understand?"

"No, sir. I mean, yes, I acknowledge the order. I don't understand it, sir."

"It was just a test. I never wanted anyone killed, but you had to approach the alien thinking I did. David, are you within earshot?"

David squeezed between the two guards and came up next to Stockwell, who backed away a step. "Right here," he said.

Lamott grinned at him. "Sorry for the melodrama, but it was the only thing I could think of. When did he become aware of the threat?"

David took a deep breath and vetoed what he wanted to say, saying instead, "When the sergeant entered the building."

"Did you notice any unusual behavior beforehand? Anything that would indicate he was aware of the danger?"

"You were talking to him yourself right up to the moment he picked up on it."

"I'm asking for your impression."

David looked over at Stockwell, who didn't seem any happier than he did, then back at the phone screen with Lamott's disembodied head in it. At that moment he would gladly have disembodied the head for real, but he just said, "I didn't notice anything unusual until Harxae said my old friend had betrayed us."

Lamott frowned. "Look, I'm sorry, but I've got national security to think of. You're asking me to try to get the brass to commit our entire planet to the riskiest thing we've ever done mostly on the strength of your word. I'm trying to verify what parts of your story I can."

"I see."

"You don't, or you wouldn't be so pissed."

David reached out with a lightning-fast finger and rapped the phone screen. Sure enough, Lamott jumped back, because on his side it looked like David was going for his throat. "You sent an armed soldier into the building with orders to kill me and my friends and you don't expect me to be pissed? What if you hadn't caught him in time?"

Lamott said, "He's got a direct command link in his helmet."

And if that had failed? David glanced over at the intensive-care room. Harxae still stood behind the window. Raedawn was in the doorway with her hands on her hips, the laser nowhere in evidence. Behind her, Boris's regenerator stood open like a clamshell, Boris himself out of sight. It took David a second to realize that one of the bed rails was missing. Not much of a weapon against an assault rifle, but he still wouldn't want to walk through that doorway just now even so.

Lamott said, "Look, it worked, okay? And now we know Harxae's range."

"And now we know what kind of person you've become, too." David rapped the screen again, but this time Lamott didn't flinch.

"Get some rest," Lamott said. "It's been a long day. Things will look better after a good night's sleep."

"Maybe. We'll see."

Lamott opened his mouth to say something more, then apparently thought better of it. He looked down at something on his desk, then back at the screen. "I'll have someone show you to your quarters. We can talk again tomorrow."

"Sure." David turned away before the screen went blank. He gave Sergeant Stockwell a questioning look, then shook his head and went back to the door. "Boris, you can put that down now."

Boris dropped to the floor; he had apparently been standing on one toe like a rock climber on the door's middle hinge pin, holding his entire body up above bullet level for someone standing in the doorway with a gun. And he had done that in Earth gravity with three broken ribs and a hip that had been dislocated just a couple of hours ago. Boris set the chrome bed rail against the wall, then climbed onto his bed again and rolled into the regenerator. "Could someone get nurse to check settings before I turn it back on?" he asked. "I think I disturb them when removing."

"Right," said David. He beckoned one of the nurses over.

Raedawn said to Harxae, "You promised to teach me how to kill anything. Let's start with Lamott."

Harxae said nothing, but David saw the corners of his mouth curl upward. So Kalirae could smile; that was another piece of information about them that Lamott didn't know.

David and Raedawn were given adjoining rooms in the VIP barracks. It was actually more of a hotel than a barracks, with comfortable furniture, a well-stocked bar in each room, and big windows overlooking a garden full of flowers and manicured ornamental trees.

David immediately stripped off his clothing and showered, then dressed in fresh pants and an aloha shirt from his duffel bag and went down to the restaurant. The closet held a dress uniform in his size, but he'd be damned if he would wear it after today.

He had a great meal of steak and buttered vegetables, savoring the first beef he'd had since going to Mars. He also savored the chance to relax by himself for a while. Raedawn and Boris were okay company, he supposed, but he wasn't used to having companions for an entire day at a stretch, especially not a day like this one. He needed the time alone to decompress.

Apparently so did Raedawn. He half expected to see her in the restaurant, but she didn't show up, and when he got back to his room he could smell some kind of curry from next door. She had ordered room service.

He lay back on his bed and stared at the ceiling as the nebulous "Tkona" went down and the sky darkened. He turned sideways and looked at the disk of planets trapped here in this pocket universe, more an airy scattered line of bright dots than a disk from Earth's point of view. The Moon was the only one that showed any detail. So much to study and learn and no time to do it in. Not if he was going to make good on his vow to bring Earth home again.

The enormity of the project threatened to overwhelm him whenever he thought about it all at once. He had to take it a piece at a time in order to believe it was possible. But he had to believe it was possible. If he didn't, then where did it leave him? Stranded back on Earth—a planet that hadn't much suited him the first time around—in a place that wasn't even part of the same universe where he was born.

All he wanted was a place to call home, a place that wasn't caught up in war or overpopulated with indifferent idiots too busy eking out their miserable existence to look up at the night sky. Earth would never be that place, but it could support colonies that might be if he could put it back where it belonged.

If. Tomorrow he would try to convince the right people that he knew what he was talking about, but tonight he would relax. He would be useless if he didn't get some rest.

He heard little noises coming from Raedawn's side of the wall. Music, occasional footsteps, running water. The connecting door between their rooms drew his attention, fueling a brief fantasy. What if he were to open his half of that door, knock on Raedawn's half, and invite her over? They had a million good excuses to talk. They should plan their strategy, both for the project and in case Lamott tried something else to test them. Talk. Or not talk.

He snorted in self-conscious derision. The odds of that happening were about as slim as the odds of moving the Earth. If Raedawn knew what he was thinking, she would laugh herself silly. Or use that little spy laser of hers to cut him to shreds. Not that she would need to. She could do the job just as well with her tongue.

Wrong image. He got up from the bed, embarrassed now, and paced the length of the room and back. Why had Lamott given them adjoining rooms, anyway? The answer was obvious: he didn't know if they were sleeping together or not, so he'd given them the option if they wanted to. How considerate of him.

The sneaky bastard.

Before he could talk himself out of it, David snatched open his half of the door and rapped on Raedawn's side.

"What?" came her muffled voice.

"Can I come in for a minute?" he asked.

"Why?"

Dare he say it out loud? He didn't see that he had much choice. "Because we're probably being monitored and if this door doesn't open at least once tonight, Lamott is going to think we're not an item, and he's going to hound you like you wouldn't believe."

"I can take care of myself."

He almost closed his door, but instead took a deep breath and said, "I know you can. But did it ever occur to you that I may not want Lamott to think we aren't an item?"

She was silent for a long few seconds. Then the door opened and she stood before him in a soft blue sweat suit, her hair freshly washed, face freshly scrubbed, and her green eyes as wide open as he'd ever seen them.

"Just what do you mean by that?" she asked.

"What do you think I mean?"

"I don't know. Why don't you tell me what you mean?"

"I thought I just did."

"I must have missed it. The double negative was kind of confusing."

Raedawn admitting to confusion? Impossible. That left only one other interpretation, which seemed equally impossible, but he was in too deep to back out now. "You're saying you want me to try something more positive?"

"I think so." She tilted her head to the side, a little smile playing across her lips. "Yeah, sure."

He hadn't been aware how hard his heart was beating until now. His skin must be bright red. He felt like he was going to burst into flame at any moment, but he leaned forward to kiss her.

He expected her to meet him halfway, but she just stood there, that damnable smile on her face, while he drew closer, waiting for her to say something snide. She said nothing, but she was going to make him go the whole distance.

So he went the whole distance. At least she didn't back away. And when their lips met, she finally relented and kissed him. She slipped her arms around his waist and pulled him against her, running her hands up and down his back.

"Do, I, um, do I make myself clear enough now?" he asked softly.

"Mmm," she said. "I don't know. Better repeat yourself just to make sure."

So he did. It turned into quite a statement. In fact, it quickly became a two-way conversation, without a doubt the best one he'd ever had with her. Her tongue turned out to be not nearly as sharp as he'd expected. In fact, there didn't seem to be a rough spot anywhere on her body.

The door remained open the rest of the night.

18

Morning arrived far too quickly. David heard the shower running when he woke, briefly considered joining Raedawn there, but decided against it. If she'd wanted company, she'd have asked.

She certainly hadn't been shy about asking for things last night. Not just physical requests, either. She seemed to think that baring his body to her also meant he should bare his soul, and she had worn him out with questions. When he'd complained she'd said, "I'm an intelligence officer. I want to know what makes you tick."

"So do I," he'd replied. "If you figure it out, clue me in, okay?"

She had proceeded to tell him what she already knew. He was driven by an urge to learn everything he could, probably because he sensed his own mortality and couldn't bear to die without knowing how the universe worked. He was offended by stupidity, impressed by ambition, and attracted to eccentricity. He thought of himself as painfully mundane and hated himself for it, but thought that cultivating an unusual lifestyle of his own would be an affectation. His extreme rationality made him feel like a misfit wherever he went. He wanted desperately to belong, but thought it was probably impossible to do so. Therefore, feeling no sense of truly belonging anywhere, he had gone to Mars when ordered to, even though he had secretly wanted to do it all along. And he had admitted his feelings for Raedawn only when he had been afraid of losing her to someone else.

"No," he'd said, "I admitted them the moment I realized I had them, which was about a millisecond before I knocked on your door."

"Bullshit," she'd said. "You've had the hots for me since you first met me. You didn't act until you thought Lamott might intrude."

Not liking the direction the conversation was going, he'd tickled her in the ribs. That had worked wonderfully, though one of his feather pillows would never be the same again.

Nor would David. In the clear light of day, he was forced to realize that her assessment of him was essentially true. She'd hit the mark on what drove him, and it was a wonder he hadn't realized all this himself before now. What he would do with the information now that she had set him straight was still a mystery, but at least he'd no longer be acting in ignorance.

He heard the shower turn off, and a moment later Raedawn came back into the room, toweling off but making no special effort to protect her modesty. He was amazed at what a night of intimacy could do. Yesterday he would have been tongue-tied in her presence, but today he merely smiled and said, "So do I want to move the Earth because I need the external validation of my genius, or do I want to do it because I'm such an altruist?"

"Neither," she said. "You want to do it because it's a scientific puzzle."

"Oh."

"And because you want to impress me."

"You think?"

"Possibly. Why else did you invite me along?"

"I think it was Kuranda's idea, actually."

She shrugged and began rubbing her hair dry. "Huh. Well, so much for that theory."

He swung his legs over the side of the bed and stood up. She eyed him appreciatively as he walked toward her, but when he tried to kiss her she backed away and said, "Let's make one thing very clear right from the start. If I wanted little smooches in the hallway, I'd have gotten married years ago. I'm not a hold-your-hand, sit-in-your-lap kind of person. If you want to play airlock, I'm all for it, but there'd better be some promise in it, okay?"

"Okay." He put his arms around her, lifted her off the ground, and kissed her in the air, but in his disoriented afterglow he had forgotten the gravity and nearly dropped her.

"What was that supposed to be?" she asked, catching herself on the door frame.

"Romantic," he said. "Let's call it a promise of romance instead. Once I get used to weighing three times what I should, I'll do that right."

"It's a deal."

She turned away, so he went into his own bathroom and showered. When he came out she was dressed again, once more in black. Her leather jacket with its little silver zippers and chains flashed under the overhead light when she moved, and her short, dark hair that fell almost but not quite into her eyes gave her an air of casual indifference that made her at once irresistible and unapproachable.

"How do you do that?" he asked her.

"What?"

"Project that 'don't touch' look."

"It's an art."

"*Why* do you do it?"

She shrugged. "I like to keep people off balance."

"You manage that. I don't know whether to haul you caveman-style back to bed or run for my life."

"Good. There should always be a little mystery in life."

He was still trying to decide whether he should advance or retreat when there was a knock at the door. Raedawn immediately stepped into her room and closed her half of the adjoining door, then popped it right back open, snatched up her sweat suit from the chair by the door, and closed it again.

David closed his side and said in a loud voice, "In a minute."

"It's Lamott."

"In that case, it'll be an hour or so." He unzipped his bag and found a pair of shorts.

"Very funny. Open up."

"Oh, all right." David did a little dance step climbing into his shorts on the way to the door, unlocked it, and stepped back as Lamott pushed his way in.

The general was not in a good mood. "You lied to me."

"I probably did," said David. "Which one did you catch?"

"What? How many lies did you tell?"

"There wouldn't be much use in lying if I revealed 'em all the moment you ask, now, would there?" David grinned. He was playing for the audience on the other side of the door as well as for Lamott. Apparently a little of Raedawn's attitude had rubbed off on him during the night, and he was surprised to discover that he liked it.

Lamott stood with his legs slightly apart and his hands behind his back as if addressing a platoon of soldiers.

"Shortly after the Change, a Neo-Sov ship crash-landed on the Moon. Its pilot, one Brygan Nystolov, followed Earth through the anomaly all the way from Mars. He says there was no alliance with your forces in the works at the time he left, and no indication that there would ever be one. In fact, until he left Mars, his orders were to find and destroy your secret base."

David shrugged nonchalantly and reached into the closet for the uniform there. He could tell he would need it today. "If this Nutsonov guy left Mars before the anomaly hit, of course he wouldn't know about the alliance. It didn't happen until after Earth had disappeared."

"Who proposed it, and under what authority? How did you negotiate the treaty? Did you bring the document with you? What about—"

"Colonel Kuranda called General Shtavyrik at the Baskurgan base on Ascraeus Mons because we believed Earth had been destroyed. We staged an attack on Tithonium Base to prove we were still a threat, then sued for peace from a position of strength."

David dressed as he spoke. The uniform was a surprisingly good fit; apparently someone had looked up his size rather than just guessed. "They resisted at first, so we shut down their communications satellites, effectively isolating their colonies from one another. When we put them back on-line a few minutes later, they were ready to talk."

Lamott wiggled his fingers nervously. "Documents?"

"They were still being drawn up when we left. We intended to wait until we received them before following Earth through the spatial anomaly, but we were sucked in before that happened."

"I don't believe a word of it."

David adjusted his tie. He hated the constricting things,

just as he hated lying like this. "Of course you don't believe me, but that doesn't really matter, does it? It makes a good story. It provides an excellent excuse to cooperate. Does it really matter if it's true or not?"

"Of course it matters! If we try to make peace with the Soviets here based on a fiction, the whole thing could fall apart in an instant."

"And exactly how would we be any worse off afterward than we are now?"

"Huh?"

"We're at war with them now. Any reason for a cease-fire is a good thing, isn't it? Especially if it lets us do what we have to do to put the Earth back where it belongs."

Lamott said, "You're not much of a strategist, are you? We've got at least a dozen separate operations under way in Neo-Soviet territory. We're taking out their munitions depots, power plants, military bases—you name it. We're not going to propose a cease-fire until it's in our best interest to do so."

"So you're saying you'd actually rather *not* have evidence of a peace treaty on Mars."

"Not right away."

"Hmm." David knocked on the door between his room and Raedawn's. "Hey, are you decent in there?" he called out.

"Yeah."

"The general's here, and he brought us a present."

He opened the door just as both Lamott and Raedawn said, "A present?"

"A wet blanket."

Raedawn opened her door and stepped into the room. "How thoughtful. What kind of . . . fire are we dousing with it?"

"Now wait a minute," Perry blustered. "You're the ones who lied to *me*. You didn't really expect me to accept your story without checking the facts, did you?"

"I don't think the facts have much to do with it," said David. "You got orders from above not to interrupt their little war, and this is your way of laying the blame on us so we won't protest."

Lamott blinked. His eyes shifted to Raedawn and back to David again, just a little flicker of motion, but it was enough.

"Hah! Guilty as charged. All right, now that we've established the truth in this conversation, let's talk reality. How long before you *can* propose a cease-fire?"

Lamott leaned back against the wall. "Maybe a week."

"We don't know the anomaly will stick around for a week."

"Well, you'll have to make sure it does. Like I told you yesterday, we need proof-of-concept anyway before we can sell this idea to either side. You'll have to go back out there and show us you can manipulate that thing. Stretch it out toward Earth, get a spectral analysis, see if you can split it in two, all that stuff. We'll try to finish up what we need to do here as quickly as we can, but we're not backing down while we're winning."

"Amazing," said David. "The Union would rather fight a war than negotiate a fragile peace."

"You attacked Tithonium before you negotiated with Shtavyrik," Lamott pointed out. "At least you said you did."

"We did," David said. That part of his story, at least, was true. "But I argued against that, too."

"No offense, but I'm amazed anyone ever thought you'd make a good scientific leader in occupied territory."

"No offense, but I'm surprised anyone ever thought

you'd make a good leader, period. You should have stuck to blowing up physics labs." David picked up his travel bag and started stuffing his belongings into it, including his dirty clothes. One sock was dangling from the bedside lamp; he saw Lamott roll his eyes when he noticed it there.

"You really haven't changed much, have you?" Lamott said.

David wasn't about to tell him how that sock had really gotten there. Let him think what he liked.

Lamott turned to Raedawn. "He used to be the sloppiest lab tech on campus. Total quark head. Couldn't keep track of his tools, busted half his equipment before he even switched it on, spilled reagents all over the floor—but he always got the best results of any of us. We all thought he fudged his data, but he could repeat everything within half a standard deviation anytime you asked him to."

"Is there a point to this homey little reminiscence?" she asked.

He sighed. "Look, I've managed to piss both of you off, and I'm sorry. I'd like to back up and start over again, but it would wind up the very same way because my responsibilities would still be to the same people. The point I'm trying to make is that I trust David. Not the story about some happy little alliance on Mars, but I trust his science. I mean that, David. If anybody could do what you're proposing, you can. I'm behind you on that all the way."

"You've got a funny way of showing it."

"And you've got a funny way of asking for help. If you had approached anybody else, you'd have been laughed right back to Mars."

"You *are* sending me back into space again," David noted, hefting his travel bag.

"To prove to everybody else that this will work. While

you're doing that, I'll lay the groundwork down here. When you get back, we can make it happen."

"That's—well, that's more encouraging than before." David looked to Raedawn. "So, um, you want to come with me or stay here?"

The question seemed to hang in the air for hours. Her eyes met his, and he saw the glint of malice that a mouse sees when the cat knows the mouse is cornered. He saw her nostrils flare and her pale white skin turn just a tiny shade redder. He saw her lips move an infinitesimal fraction of a millimeter and he knew she was going to laugh; he could hear her voice say, *Hah! You think I'd go back into danger for you?*

Sure enough, when she finally spoke, she said, "Are you kidding?" He felt the knife blade slide into his chest, but the wound healed without a trace when she finished her thought: "I wouldn't miss it for the world."

"So to speak," said Lamott, who seemed blissfully unaware of the near-death experience he had just witnessed.

David remembered to breathe again. "Well, then. Once more into the breach, and all that."

"So to speak," Raedawn said; and this time the twinkle in her eyes was unmistakable.

19

oris and Harxae were not coming along on this trip. Boris wasn't going anywhere for at least a week, and Union Command wasn't about to let Harxae out of sight until they learned everything they could from him about the Earth's new environment. That process wouldn't begin until they knew more about his telepathic ability, but they preferred to keep him under wraps so the Neo-Soviets couldn't capture him and benefit from his knowledge.

David shook his head in disgust when he heard that. He still couldn't believe that a planetary crisis of this magnitude would fail to pull humanity together for the common good, but it hadn't happened on Mars and it hadn't happened here, either.

He once again wondered if humanity was worth saving, but he reminded himself that there must be a few grandmothers and innocent children left in the world. Besides, he had committed himself to saving Earth and he wasn't about to back out now.

Lamott couldn't spare a full-sized warship for a scientific expedition, but he provided them with a new shuttle and a gunner to help place the EMP bombs near the nebula—and to help defend the ship from any more hostile aliens who might come to investigate. David wasn't sure he wanted the company, then knew he didn't when he found out the identity of that soldier: Sergeant Stockwell, the one Lamott had sent to the hospital yesterday to assassinate David and his crew.

Stockwell was already on board when they arrived. At least he was no longer in battle armor. He wore plain brown fatigues today, and the only hand weapon in evidence was the data pad he carried while he ran a systems check and supervised missile stowage. The ship was carrying an entire cargo hold full of pulse bombs, low-yield nuclear warheads not particularly useful as explosives but excellent for disrupting electronics. And, if David's theory was correct, just the thing for luring what was left of the anomaly toward Earth again. They were rack-mounted for sequential launching without having to reload the launch tubes manually—a big improvement over the impromptu design they had cobbled together on the shuttle.

The moment Sergeant Stockwell saw David, he stiffened and said, "*Sir!* Welcome aboard, sir. I'm sorry about yesterday, sir." Then he saw Raedawn coming up the ramp behind him and amended that to "Sirs."

"Me, too," said David. He noted that the sergeant didn't apologize for what he'd done, which he couldn't very well do since he'd been following orders, but he'd still managed to apologize. Nicely done. Maybe this guy wouldn't be so bad after all. He said, "If we're going to be sharing a ship for a few days, I think we'd better dispense with all the 'sirs.' I'm David, and this is Raedawn."

"I'm Rick." He smiled and extended his hand to shake. "Thank you, s—uh, thanks."

"Don't let the uniform throw you off," said David. "I

thought I'd be trying to impress the brass today, but I normally don't stand on protocol."

"That's, uh, that'll be refreshing, sir. David."

Raedawn laughed. "Sir David. Earth's knight in shining armor. I don't know, but I think you look kind of buff in a uniform."

David didn't know what to say to that. Neither did Rick. He didn't seem to know what to do with his hands all of a sudden, but finally settled on waving toward the interior of the ship. "Why don't you stow your things while I finish the preflight?"

"Good idea."

This ship was big enough to have a separate deck for the control cabin and crew quarters. Raedawn waited until they had laboriously climbed the stairs before she said, "He's cute."

"He's nervous. And he's just a kid. Don't you start giving him the kind of grief you give me."

"Grief? Me?"

"You."

There were two doors on either side of a narrow corridor, and one at the end. All five stood open. The control cabin lay beyond the far door, the one on the left behind that held a galley that looked like it had been lifted straight out of a suborbital passenger shuttle. The other three were tiny staterooms about two meters on a side, just big enough for a bed and a locker. The one behind the galley had a hat lying in the middle of the bed, which left the two on the right. There were no adjoining doors, David noted.

"Take your pick," he said.

"Like there's much difference." She tossed her bag into the forward one, then went into the control cabin and settled into the pilot's chair and started examining the controls. "Oh, this is better. I'll just live in here."

There were three seats side by side, and enough switches, dials, displays, and touchpads to satisfy even the most devout gadget-head. David noted the layout and tried to commit as much to memory as he could, then he looked up and saw the entire ceiling covered with more readouts and control panels.

"I've seen simpler systems. You know what all this stuff does?"

Raedawn reached upward and flipped a couple of toggles over her head, and suddenly David felt as if he were falling.

"Yow!" he yelped, grabbing the door frame for support.

"Yep," said Raedawn. She slowly increased the gravity again, but left it at Mars normal. "Careful on the stairs. I left it Earth normal down below. Didn't want to give Rick any grief, you know."

"You're so sweet." David tossed his bag onto the remaining bunk and went back down to see what he could do to help.

They were in space within the hour. Raedawn piloted from the center seat, with Rick on her left and David on her right. With internal agrav to compensate for the thrust, she boosted at eight gees, tearing out of the atmosphere almost as quickly as they had entered it. At least this time the air grew thinner as their velocity increased, and by the time the hull grew dangerously hot they were in vacuum and radiating it away again.

There were no ships in pursuit this time, either.

"Next stop, the Sol nebula," she said as she targeted the glowing white cloud and engaged the autopilot. "At least we're assuming that's what it is," she said for Rick's benefit.

"That much we can check from here," said David. He scanned the panel in front of him for the telescope controls, finally found them next to the communications panel, and zoomed in on the nebula. It was much smaller than before, barely the size of the Moon now, and not nearly as active as it had been. He called up a spectral analysis of it, then called up the solar spectrum from the navigation computer's memory. They matched perfectly, with the exception of some absorption lines from the nebula.

"I'll be damned," he said. "There's actually matter involved. I thought it was all magnetic and quantum effects."

"Isn't that what matter is?" Raedawn asked.

"Well, yeah, down at the fundamental level. I just didn't expect to see that kind of effect here. I wonder if we can tell what kind of matter it is."

It took a few minutes to run the spectral analysis, but when it popped up on the screen, it contained enough surprises to be worth the wait. There was quite a bit of nitrogen and oxygen, which was to be expected since the Earth's atmosphere had been so violently disturbed on the way through, but there were also strong lines from iron, aluminum, and copper, plus traces of carbon, hydrogen, sodium, potassium, and a dozen lesser compounds.

"Air, metals, and carbon," David mused. "That looks to me like a space station or a ship that didn't make it through."

"I'm sure there were plenty of those," said Rick. "Our base alone sent two ships back into it after we got here. I'm sure other people must have tried, too, until they realized nobody was coming back to report success."

David tried to estimate how much mass they were dealing with based on the strength of the absorption lines and the size of the nebula. He came up with somewhere between a million and ten million kilograms, which seemed within reason for maybe a hundred ships and satellites and other hardware. With an order of magnitude, anyway, which was about all he could expect with such a rough measurement.

The military ship was far faster than their shuttle had been. At full thrust it only took two hours to reach the nebula. Raedawn brought them to a stop a hundred thousand kilometers away, much closer to it than the Moon was to Earth, but it had shrunk so much that it still looked like a tiny white shred of cloud that had been left behind on a summer afternoon.

David measured it at less than a thousand klicks across. It had been shrinking at about twelve per hour as they approached. Their presence had slowed it by a couple percent, but not as much as he had expected.

"All right," he said. "First let's see if we can stop that contraction completely. What do you think of four pulse bombs at the corners of a tetrahedron around it?"

"It's a start," Raedawn said.

"Rick? You want to do the honors?"

"Sure." Rick got busy at his weapons control screens, and a minute later the ship rocked as four missiles streaked away. Raedawn canceled the ship's motion, and they waited as the missiles approached their targets.

"Should I shut down the drive, or do you think the magnetic effects will matter from this distance?"

"Leave it hot," said David. "If it does matter, I want to see how much. But get ready to shut it down if it matters a lot."

"Right."

He called up a magnetic field map of the nebula. Like the map he'd seen when it swallowed Earth, it was a snarl of intense field lines, swirling around chaotically like a dynamo that had slipped its bearings.

The missiles continued on, their rocket flames drawing tiny star-bright points against the gray background that bounded the pocket universe. They were the only four stars in the sky, and the only ones likely to be there until they blew open the anomaly again.

"Coming up on position," Rick reported. "Detonation in five . . . four . . . three . . . two . . . one."

All four charges went off simultaneously, three in an equilateral triangle just beyond the nebula and one directly in front of it. They were just tiny white flashes at this distance, but David saw the magnetic effects on his screen. Four tight swirls of magnetism swelled outward, and four buds immediately stretched out from the nebula toward them. Within seconds the nebula went from roughly spherical to obviously triangular. David checked the distance readings and saw that the center had bulged out toward them—and was still coming.

"Hold steady. Our presence is definitely having an effect."

He switched from the magnetic view to the optical one. It was hard to see the forward motion, since the thing was coming straight toward them, but the three points on the side kept billowing outward, their shapes smoothing out again from angular points to semicircular growths, like ears.

"Mickey Mouse," he said. "It looks like Mickey Mouse."

"With Pinocchio's nose," Raedawn added.

The center was still coming. David checked its velocity; twenty kilometers per second, but it increased to twenty-one as he watched.

"Shut down the drive," he said.

Raedawn did. The lights blinked as the ship went on battery power. David kept his eye on the screen, watching the velocity figure blink up to twenty-two, hold steady for a minute or so, then fall, but not by much.

"Man, it's touchy," he said. "Let's see if we can split it in two. How about a string of three bombs on either side of it, timed to blow in sequence just as the leading edge reaches them."

"I can do that," said Rick. His fingers flew over the tactical screens, and a minute later six missiles sped away.

A few minutes after that, the bombs exploded one after the other like two strings of landing lights leading in opposite directions. The nebula had grown toward the ship like a snake; now it grew two horns. White cloudscape ballooned out to either side, engulfing one field of bomb debris after the other, but the middle kept coming forward.

"It doesn't want to split," David said. "That tells us something."

"What?" Raedawn asked.

"Well, that it doesn't want to split, for starters. There's some kind of cohesiveness to it. Either the magnetic field is holding it together, or there's some other effect we're not aware of." He noted the approach velocity, which had not dropped more than a few meters per second. "There seems to be a nearly infinite supply of it, too. The ears in back are slowly drawing toward us as the front side stretches out, but producing those side spikes hardly affected the forward propagation at all."

"Now what?" asked Rick.

"Well," said David. "We're supposed to lead the thing back to Earth. Let's nudge ourselves back in that direction and see if it keeps following us."

"Nudge?" Raedawn asked. "It's coming toward us at

over three times orbital velocity. I'll have to use the main engines for almost four minutes to match that."

"Four minutes? You're kidding." David did the calculation in his head. Twenty kilometers per—"Oh shit. *Kilometers.*" He'd been thinking meters. It was coming at them a thousand times faster than he had thought.

20

They had two options. They could remain where they were and hope that the nebula would stop expanding before it reached them, or run now and hope to out-accelerate it. David did a quick calculation of how long it would take to come to rest again at its current rate of deceleration and came up with nearly two hours. They were an hour and a half away at its current speed. If it slowed at more than a few meters per second squared it might stop before it reached them. But the closer it came, the more it would feel even the minor magnetic effects from the ship that couldn't be shielded without shutting down everything, including the air scrubbers. He didn't want to sit there for two hours waiting to see what would happen while his air slowly ran out.

"Get us out of here," he said. "Maximum acceleration."

"Roger." Raedawn warmed up the drive again, firing the injectors the moment the pinch field had stabilized. She swirled the ship around under acceleration, carving out a fuel-wasting arc in space, but that was faster than turning first and then lighting the engine. David was glad for the artificial gravity; in the shuttle, that maneuver would have flattened everyone.

He switched to the aft view. The nebula didn't react for a second, then he realized that was the speed-of-light lag he was seeing. The moment the ship's magnetic field had intensified, the nebula had sensed it, and the forward edge leaped toward them.

"Twenty-one klicks per second," he called out. Six seconds ticked by. "Twenty-two." Another six seconds. "Twenty-three."

"At least it isn't accelerating as fast as it did toward the bombs," Rick said.

"It's fast enough," said Raedawn. "We're doing fifteen gees. It's doing what, sixteen?"

"About that," said David.

"At this rate, it'll catch us when?"

"Call it an hour and a half. Maybe less."

"Right about the time we get to Earth," Rick said. "Assuming we lead it that direction."

"We can't," said Raedawn. "They aren't ready for us." She changed their angle, aiming for empty space well above the plane of captured planets.

That was true enough. David wondered how long it would take them to get ready. At least a week to finish up their little war, and an indefinite time after that to convince everyone that it was possible, then an indefinite time after that to squabble about whether or not it should be done at all, and so on for months. Maybe even years. There was no way they could keep this anomaly stable that long. The very physical laws that governed it seemed to shift from moment to moment. Sometimes it was attracted by small magnetic fields, and sometimes it took pulse bombs to get its attention. What if it suddenly decided to ignore everything they did and close up once and for all?

"On the other hand," he said, "what does Earth really need to do? We thought we'd need EMP bombs all over the planet to attract the anomaly, but it's obvious we don't. If we keep shooting ours out farther and farther to the side as we go, it'll be as big as the Earth-Moon system by the time we get there."

Raedawn said, "And what happens then? We don't want to just hit the Earth with it; we have to be ready to blow it open, too."

"They've got the firepower," David said. "They're using it to blow each other up at the moment, but it's deployed all over the planet and in space, too. It would be just as easy to coordinate an attack on *that* as it would on each other." He rapped on the rapidly expanding white cloud on the telescope screen.

Raedawn ran her left hand through her hair. "They're not going to like you forcing their hand."

"They're not going to do anything if we don't," David pointed out.

"Do you really think that's a decision you can make on the spur of the moment like this?"

David's voice was urgent. "The Pentagon doesn't want us to spoil their war, and I don't imagine the Soviets do, either. Both sides are in it too deep to back out gracefully. They'll keep stalling and stalling until it's too late. Don't you see? This may be our only chance."

Raedawn nodded slightly, still considering it.

Rick was growing more and more nervous in the seat between them. "Um, sirs?" he said finally. "I think I'd better tell you that I have orders to stop you if you try to do anything that will endanger the Earth without General Lamott's authorization."

David focused on the soldier's face. Drops of sweat were forming on his forehead. "You do, eh?"

"Yes, sir."

"Then we'll have to make sure we don't endanger the Earth, 'cause I can practically guarantee you Lamott won't authorize this."

"Um . . . how can we bring the nebula to Earth without endangering it? Last time we went through it, there were earthquakes and storms and—"

"It's a matter of degree," David said. "Sending the planet back through there is going to be dangerous, no doubt of that. But leaving it here is even more so. Look out there." He pointed out the forward windows at the vast expanse of planets beyond Earth.

"It's probably only a matter of time before an asteroid too big to deflect smacks into Earth. Or maybe another whole planet. And even if we get lucky in that regard, Harxae says everything eventually spirals into the center anyway."

He rapped on the screen showing the nebula that pursued them. "And if we let that shrink to nothing, there'll be no going back to the solar system ever again. That's our only link with home. Even if we manage to punch our way out into normal space again, without that link, we could wind up anywhere."

He watched Raedawn as well as Rick while he spoke. Neither of them looked convinced, but they were both thinking about it.

"What if we just drag the anomaly close for now and give them time to prepare before we actually hit 'em with it?" Rick asked.

"Can we do that?" Raedawn asked David.

"No. Well, actually, we can drag it anywhere we want if it doesn't quit responding to us in the way it has, but it's going to hit *us* no matter what."

All three were silent for a moment.

David finally said, "Look, I don't think I want to let that thing possibly kill us for nothing. We haven't come this far to just disappear into the black without at least trying to complete what we set out to do."

Rick swallowed hard. "So we know it's only a matter of time before that thing catches up with us. But won't we be able to get back out again? Earth did. You guys did."

Raedawn shook her head. "We came *through* one. Maybe we could get back out, but maybe not. The missile the Kalirae shot into our little mini-anomaly went in, but it just stretched the other side out until it came to a stop. I get the feeling these things are one-way doors."

David nodded. "One way, and we're trying to go the wrong way, which is why we have to blow up the door we come through once we're inside. But it's the only chance we've got."

Rick looked at him, then at Raedawn. He bit his lower lip, then said, "We'll all be court-martialed if this doesn't work."

"We'll probably be dead if this doesn't work," Raedawn said.

Rick looked to David for confirmation.

"She's right."

He swallowed again. "So what do we tell Earth?"

Raedawn let out a harsh laugh. "How about, '*Duck!*' "

"That ought to just about cover it," David said, feeling himself relax slightly at the realization that they were going to go for his idea. The thought of going into danger didn't bother him nearly as much as the thought of missing their only opportunity to save the world.

They all exchanged quick nods and began to prepare. He felt a thrill of excitement run up his spine as Raedawn brought their flight path back in line with Earth.

"We'd better get busy expanding this thing so it takes in the whole Earth-Moon system when it gets there," he said, "or we'll do more harm than good. Rick, what do you say to shots of three EMPs at a time, placed at the points of an equilateral triangle for maximum spread per bomb? How many shots would that give us?"

"We loaded a hundred even. I've got ninety left, so we could do thirty spreads."

"Once every six minutes, then. That's *explosion* time, not launch time. We'll have to launch 'em closer and closer together toward the end because they'll have farther to travel."

"Right. I'm on it." He started work, firing the first three after just a few seconds of calculation, then working on the next shot, and the next.

David watched until he was sure it was going to work. The nebula expanded with each EMP blast, but now that they had veered away from their initial path and back, he could see the backside of it, and he confirmed that it was pulling together with the front. It was a long tube now, but by the time it reached Earth it would be nearly spherical again.

Another EMP pulse stretched it out another few hundred kilometers. The ship raced onward, drawing it along behind.

He turned the telescope forward, centering it on Earth. The tiny blue-and-white planet floated serenely in space, the Moon just beyond it. David wished there was a better way to do this, but he was stuck between an onrushing space warp and a hardheaded bureaucracy.

He reached for the radio controls, turned the incoming audio all the way down, then opened a channel to Union Space Command. Then he proceeded to tell them what they had to do.

21

houldn't we, um, shouldn't we listen for orders?" Rick asked.

"What for?" David replied. "We know what we have to do. They know what they have to do. Argu—talking about it will just slow us all down."

"I'm not supposed to be out of touch with my commanding officer."

"I'm your commanding officer on board this ship, aren't I?"

"Yes, but—"

"No buts. We've thought this through, and this is the only course of action open to us. Let's just do our jobs and not worry about what people might say until we're back home." David hoped appealing to duty was the right approach. This was the guy who was willing to die yesterday to follow his orders, no matter how much he disliked them. The question was where his loyalty lay: to the military hierarchy, or to humanity.

"Twenty minutes to rendezvous," Raedawn said.

David looked at the distance and velocity figures of the nebula. "Eighteen minutes to impact."

"Are we, um, at full velocity?" Rick asked.

"Flat out," Raedawn assured him. "Don't worry; we can survive a couple of minutes inside it. I've been thinking it over and I think we're better off this way anyway. Since we're leading the anomaly to Earth, there's no way we can slow down fast enough to be alongside Earth when that thing engulfs it. So our best chance is to actually let it catch us just beforehand, and be inside of it when Earth blows their bombs."

David tried to picture that in his mind. Their ship racing toward the planet, the nebula catching up and passing them, then enveloping the Earth two minutes later. Earth would detonate every bomb they could in low orbit, and Lunar Command would do the same. They had no choice; it was either that or be stuck inside the nebula with everything merging together again until it shrank to nothing or spit them back out again. But if they fired their missiles, the shock wave would rip the nebula open, and a patch of normal space would sweep the Earth and the Moon—and their ship—back where they belonged.

Whereupon the ship would crash into the Earth at about six hundred kilometers per second.

"Uh . . . make sure we're not aimed right *at* the planet when we go in, okay?"

"Duh," she said. "I'm aimed halfway between Earth and the Moon. Otherwise we'd have to make the anomaly even bigger to hit both of 'em."

"Oh. Right."

Rick paused in his bomb-launch calculations, a thoughtful expression on his face. "What happens if the Moon and the Earth each blow separate holes in the nebula, but the middle part doesn't tear open?"

David felt a moment of panic, but then he remembered

something that calmed him back down a bit. As calm as he could be in the situation, at any rate. He said, "When the Kalirae missile blew our little one open, the whole thing burst like a soap bubble. I'm betting the big one will work the same way."

"Betting?" said Raedawn. "Can't we maybe hedge that bet a little?"

"How?"

"What if we blow our own hole in it?"

He thought that over. "We'd have to get the timing exactly right. If we blew it too soon and it *does* rip the whole thing open, we could leave the Earth or the Moon behind."

"So we wait until we're sure we're past 'em."

"We won't be able to see from inside there, and time doesn't work the same as it does out here, either. We won't know when we've passed."

"I'd say if we haven't come out in a week, we could feel pretty safe in figuring we've gone far enough," Raedawn said.

"Maybe." David stretched a kink out of his neck. "I don't know. We lost a week in a few minutes last time. Going the other way we could gain that much or more. I'd rather err on the side of caution."

"I'd rather err on the side of living through it," she said.

He nodded. "If it comes to that choice, we can make our decision then. Who knows, maybe we'll have more data to go on. But for now, let's not plan on doing anything that might screw this up."

Rick kept firing the EMP missiles, but David noted that he'd activated a separate tactical screen with six "ass-busters," which was what Space Command affectionately called the high-yield fission-fusion bombs they had developed to shatter asteroids on collision course with Earth. If anything would open a hole in the nebula, those would do it.

Raedawn looked down at her navigation display again. "Fifteen min—shit! Incoming!" She hit the attitude thrusters at full blast, rotating the ship through ninety degrees while the engines were still pouring out fifteen gees of thrust. The agravs compensated for most of it, but David felt a queasy hollowness in his stomach.

It might have been sheer terror. There was an explosion so close to the window that he felt the heat from the flash, but they were moving so fast it was gone in the blink of an eye.

"Those stupid sons of bitches," he whispered.

"Two more! Rick, can you intercept them?"

"I'll try." He already had three EMP bombs ready to fly; he canceled their programmed course and launched them straight forward. "Range?" he asked.

"Two thousand."

"Get ready to dodge again. They'll still be coming blind even if we fry 'em."

Raedawn held her hand over the attitude jet control. Rick held his over the manual detonate spot on the tactical screen.

"One thousand," she said.

"Almost there."

"Seven hundred."

He stabbed at the trigger, and an instant later three bright flashes erupted directly in front of them.

"Go!" he shouted.

Raedawn spun them another ninety degrees. They held their breaths for five or ten seconds, but when nothing hit them she turned them back on course.

David checked the nebula. "That drew it ahead even

more than our drive was doing. Impact in nine minutes now."

"There's more missiles coming!"

David switched on the radio. "What are you idiots trying to do?" he yelled. "You're not going to stop the nebula even if you hit us! And if you hit *it,* you're liable to blow it open too soon."

He heard a tiny voice buzzing furiously in the console and turned up the volume in time to hear "—what we're trying to do, you stupid son of a bitch!"

"Negative! Don't do that! It's your only chance to get home. You've got to blow it right on top of you, not before!"

"That's what you think. We're not going through that thing again!" In the background they could hear another voice shout, "Fire! Fire everything you've got!"

"Jesus H. Christ," David said, switching off the radio again. "What can we do?"

Raedawn and Rick both looked at him with stunned expressions.

"We can't let them blow it up early."

They still said nothing.

"Come on, think! There's another wave of missiles on the way. If they get past us, we're all stranded here forever."

Rick looked back at his tactical screen. "We've still got eighteen pulse bombs. What if we shot them straight ahead like the last three? Send them all out in a line and fire them in sequence toward Earth? That ought to fry everything they send toward us right up to the moment of impact."

"And it would drag the nebula over us minutes early," Raedawn said.

She obviously didn't like that idea, but David said, "That might not be a problem. If they blow it early, at least *we* get to go back home. We've given them their chance; the rest is up to them."

Rick said, "The nebula isn't wide enough for both Earth and the Moon to squeeze through."

David looked at the figures on his screen. He was right. But it was close. "All right, give it two more shots, but just to the sides at this point. Draw it out in a line. Four bombs will do that. Use the rest to stop their missiles."

"Roger." Rick got to work, and the ship shuddered with more launches.

"More incoming!" Raedawn suddenly said.

Rick stabbed at the trigger for the closest bomb. It flashed like a strobe going off right in front of their eyes, and a moment later Raedawn took evasive maneuvers, but one of the missiles came through live. She veered again, then cut the power, then ran it up to full again, but she needn't have bothered. This missile wasn't aimed at the ship. It streaked on past, heading straight for the nebula.

Rick kept his eyes on his job. More flashes erupted at increasing distance, and two more winked far to the sides, drawing the nebula out ever wider.

David watched the rear 'scope screen as Raedawn brought them back on course. The nebula was racing toward them like a hurricane toward shore, and the tiny spark of the missile shot out to meet it. It disappeared into the rolling white surface, and for a moment it looked like nothing would happen, then there was a bright flash and a circle of darkness stretched out like an ink blot.

"Dammit!" David cursed. "They did it, but it's too soon!" He zoomed in on the circle even as it widened, saw the silvery twinkle of stars shining through it, and growled deep in his throat. "They blew it. They blew it!"

But the ragged hole in space stopped expanding, and a moment later it started to collapse on itself again.

"Holy shit. Raedawn, turn us around. Aim for that opening before it's gone!"

"We'd never make it," she said.

She was right. It closed with the speed of a camera iris; one moment there, the next gone.

"They didn't ruin it, though," David said in amazement. "It's resilient. We've still got a chance!"

"Do you think they'll actually take the big shot when they're supposed to, or are they going to try it early?"

"If they try it early after seeing that, then they're even more stupid than I think they are."

Even so, there were more missiles on the way, and Rick's EMP bombs had scrambled their electronics. They watched as the missiles swerved every which way, some detonating early, but others roaring deep into the nebula before ripping open more holes into normal space.

The explosions were playing hob with his calculations, but David checked the nebula's velocity one last time and said, "Impact in one minute, more or less."

"Any last words?" Raedawn asked.

He looked at her. She looked at him, her eyes reflecting Earth light, nebula light, and more.

"We're going to survive this," he said.

He didn't know what he expected from her, but whatever it was, it wasn't laughter. She leaned back and roared, then shook her head and said, "That'll look good on your tombstone."

He supposed it would at that. "Okay, I give you permission to chisel it there yourself, but only after we're both old and gray."

"Deal."

He nodded toward the window. "Aim for the next opening. To hell with waiting. We've done our job."

"My sentiments exactly." Raedawn brought the ship around, and they waited for another missile to strike. The sight of the huge wall of white cloud bearing down on them made all three of them gasp and lurch back in their chairs, and Raedawn was a second slow when a patch of blackness opened off to their left.

She recovered instantly, but the wall was upon them just as she turned the ship. They were blind just as quickly, at first in the bright fog, then in the grainy gray darkness that slowly robbed the light from around them.

Then there was a brilliant flash of light and they burst into clear space. For just an instant they saw the blackness of open space, dusted by bright points of light, then the opening snapped shut on them and they were once again in the fuzzy gray interior of the nebula.

There was another flash of light below them.

"There!" both Rick and David said.

Raedawn turned the ship toward it, but after thirty seconds or so under thrust, she throttled back the engines and said, "We missed it."

"Should we make our own?" Rick said.

"Not yet." David looked at his display. The velocity figures were meaningless now, but he remembered the last real ones before they had been swallowed up. "They still had five minutes to impact. Let's give them that much, at least. More if we can."

"Then brace for zero gee," Raedawn said.

"What?" asked Rick. "Why?"

"Because we're going to start slipping into our chairs if I don't shut it off. It's one of the things that happens in here. Things blend together."

"You're kidding."

"Nope. Last time we had to strip down and float free."

David shoved his finger against the console in front of him. When he pulled it back, there was a faint tug, but hardly more than normal. "I don't think it's as bad as it was before," he said. "It's certainly not as dark this time. Maybe the larger size of the anomaly dilutes the effect."

"Or maybe we're just not near the middle of it yet," Raedawn said. She reached overhead and flipped the toggles she had used to startle David before, and the gravity once again vanished.

Or maybe the rules had changed again. Here, there was no telling.

"Don't use the drive on full with the gravity off," David told her.

"Good point." She moved a slide control on the panel in front of her. "There. One gee max if I do."

They floated in silence for a few seconds, waiting to see what would happen next. Rick fidgeted, holding his hand up before his eyes and squinting at it through the speckled gray air. He lowered his hand and peered out the window.

"Is it my imagination, or is it getting lighter?" he finally asked.

"I think it's getting lighter," Raedawn replied.

"Got any idea which direction we're pointed?"

"I don't think it matters," David said.

"I hope not," said Raedawn. "I'd hate to—" She stopped, her mouth agape. Right in front of them, a huge black shadow loomed out of the mist.

It didn't look like the holes back into normal space that they had seen before. It looked like a flat black wall rushing toward them, a wall filled with speckles of light, but not like starlight. It looked more like patches of brightness outlining the edges of deep night. Then the mist suddenly cleared, and they saw it for what it was: city lights around rivers, lakes, and coastlines. They were about to smash into the night side of the Earth.

22

"E vasive!" David yelled, but Raedawn was already on it. She lit the engines and angled them away, then reached up and flipped the gravity back on and ran the thrust up to full.

It wasn't going to be enough. They were heading straight for the middle of the planet, and they were only seconds away from hitting it. There was no way they could dodge thousands of kilometers to the side in that short a time.

David had always heard that time seemed to telescope when death was imminent. Your life was supposed to flash before your eyes, and all your triumphs and regrets were supposed to parade past to haunt you. It didn't work that way this time. He felt his heart thud once in his chest, struggled for breath, and just had time enough to think of one thing: they had been *that* close to making it. They had actually seen clear space in the middle of the bomb blasts. Hell, they had gone through some of it.

"Wait a minute. Fire a missile!" he said.

"At Earth?" asked Rick.

"Yes, but blow it up right out of the tube. Right in front of us. Do it!"

Maybe Rick thought he meant to fragment the ship before it hit so it wouldn't do so much damage to the people below, or maybe he was just used to obeying orders without question, but he immediately launched one of the six "assbusters" and stabbed at the detonate button in the same motion. Fortunately, his finger missed the screen's hot spot on his first try, and by the time he could hit, the missile was a kilometer or so away.

The explosion was blinding just the same. Shrapnel slammed into the ship, and an ominous shriek of breathing air began to howl somewhere in back.

"Yow!" Raedawn yelled, shoving hard on throttles that were already at full extension.

"No, back off!" David said. "Shut 'em down!"

"Are you nuts?"

"Look!" He pointed out the front window. Everyone's eyes were filled with afterimages, but they could see one thing clearly enough: Earth was gone. Star-filled space extended away on all sides.

"Holy shit," Raedawn said softly. "We made it."

"But did we—did we blow up the Earth?" asked Rick.

David felt as if he were balanced on a knife blade. A moment ago they were going to die, and now—what? Something had connected in his subconscious mind, something that had made him try firing the missile, but he hadn't done it to blow up the Earth. He tried to think it through aloud. "We couldn't have. We just opened a hole between us and it. The missile wasn't big enough to shatter a planet, anyway."

"But it was big enough to shatter the nebula," Raedawn said. "We're home."

"Not for long." Rick pointed out the window. The stars were already flickering out. Dark tendrils of chaos were erupting back into space around them.

Raedawn whirled the ship around, but it was doing the same thing behind them. She tried pitching the nose up, then down, but the stars had vanished completely. The ship was surrounded, and the noose was tightening fast.

"No!" she yelled, pounding on the console in front of her.

"Should we try another missile?" asked Rick.

"Sure," David said. What did they have to lose? "One more, straight ahead. See what it does when it goes in from this side."

Rick fired one, waited with his finger above the detonator until it just reached the blackness, then blew its warhead. This time it was far enough away that the flash was merely bright. There were no more impacts, but the steady howl of air rushing into vacuum reminded them that they needed to patch the hull soon even so.

The bomb had an effect, but it was the wrong one. A tendril of energy wrapped around the blast, then shot out hundreds of lightning bolts in all directions—five or six of them disconcertingly close to the ship.

"Take us away from—" David began, but he had no chance to finish. There was no place to go. In an instant, the sphere of darkness constricted like a fist.

The ship lurched hard, even with the agrav to compensate, and the howl of air grew even more intense. David caught a flash of motion out the window, and for a moment it looked like they were surrounded by rock. Red rock, stacked in layers that rushed past faster than the eye could follow. It was just a subliminal impression, followed immediately by a flash of blue, then dark red and brown and green, then more blue. The ship shuddered and screamed.

They were tumbling. Tumbling *away* from the Earth. Roaring out of a canyon on the day side of the planet.

"Oh," he said, trying to catch his breath.

"What?" asked Rick.

"We went through it."

Raedawn and Rick both tilted their heads and narrowed their eyes in the same comic expression of disbelief. "No, really," David said. "We were about to hit it at—what?—six hundred kilometers per second? Then we slipped into another universe for twenty seconds or so. When we popped back out, we were on the other side."

The buffeting had already stopped. Raedawn scrambled to stabilize the ship and aimed their nose back along their flight path, and sure enough, there was the Earth. It already looked like an inverted blue-and-white bowl, visibly receding, with an incandescent streak of ionized atmosphere pointing straight up at their ship. Theirs had been the most spectacular—and the quickest—ground-to-orbit launch in history. Too fast to even heat up the hull, but the air they had punched through was hot enough to glow in daylight.

Rick pointed with a shaky hand. "Is that the Grand Canyon?"

Their ion trail began in the middle of a winding scar in the ground. On either end of the scar were long, contorted lakes. David had seen that sight before. "I think so."

Raedawn was breathing hard. He couldn't tell if she was about to yell at him or what. She had to swallow a couple of times just to find her voice, but when she spoke, it was surprisingly controlled. "Tell me how you knew that would work."

He didn't feel like he could take credit for it. "I wish I could, but it was just a hunch. The other little pocket universes that the missiles opened up seemed to last a few seconds each, so I guessed that a bigger blast would hold one open longer. I didn't have time to think it through. In fact, in retrospect, I think I must have been expecting us to move a lot farther while we were in regular space."

She didn't say anything, so he went on. "I mean, we weren't even aiming anywhere near Earth when we ran through that first one, and look where we wound up. But evidently that was from all the maneuvering we did inside the nebula. It looks like the distance we traveled in real space matched the Earth kilometer for kilometer."

Still no response. He realized he was babbling, but the silence was like an accusation. "We were actually very lucky," he said. "If we'd been going a little bit slower, or if we hadn't popped out in the middle of the canyon, we'd have fallen short. We would have materialized inside solid rock."

That's not what she wanted to hear. She stared at him for a few more seconds, then unbuckled her harness and got out of her chair. "I'm going to go patch that leak," she said.

"That's . . . that's a good idea."

She walked down the narrow corridor between their tiny bunkrooms and descended the stairs. When she reached the cargo hold, they heard her scream. "Aaaaaaaaaarrrrrrrgggghhhh!"

Rick immediately slapped the emergency release on his harness, but David put out a hand and held him in his chair. "Believe me, you don't want to go back there right now."

"But she—"

"She's all right. In fact, I can practically guarantee you she's doing better now than you or me. But she undoubtedly wants to be alone."

Rick sat back down. "So do I," he admitted. He looked at the Earth, now small enough to see the entire globe in the window. "Actually, I want to go home."

David hit the button that slaved the navigation controls

to his side of the console and shot Rick a shaky grin. "Let's see if there's still any chance of that."

It quickly became clear that there wasn't much hope in salvaging their original plan. The roiling white nebulosity had roared through Earth as well, or around it or past it, depending on how big a hole the Union and the Neo-Soviets had blown in it. It had passed their ship while they were inside the Earth, and the planet's magnetic field had acted like a huge lens, focusing it back into a small but intense knot of activity that shrank faster than mere recession into the distance could account for. It was already too far away for the ship's drive to have any effect on it, and shrinking too fast to catch even with an EMP missile.

David watched it go, hoping it would rebound when it reached some critical density, but he knew that was only wishful thinking. There was no density to begin with. It was all energy, a topological abstraction, an effect of twisted space and nothing more. There was nothing to stop it from collapsing completely, a fact that became evident when the roiling white nebula diminished from a planet-swallower to a thundercloud to a weather balloon to a golf ball . . . to nothing.

He trained the telescope on the space where it had been and ran the magnification all the way up, but he saw only distant planets and the Tkona beyond them.

"That," he said, "was the sight of our doom and our last hope both vanishing at once."

The howl of leaking air changed pitch, then a moment later stopped altogether. He looked back over his shoulder. "Since we're still breathing, I guess we're probably going to live a while longer. Yee-ha."

Rick didn't reply to that. The tone of David's voice

didn't leave much room for response. When Rick did speak, it was to say, "I've got a wife and a son back on Earth."

"Oh." David had been on his own so long he'd forgotten what it felt like to have family.

"What am I going to tell them?" Rick asked.

David turned the ship back toward Earth and lit the drive. It would take a while to cancel their velocity, and a while longer to go back the other way. "I guess I'd tell 'em to carpe that old diem. Live each day like it was your last, because it may very well be. Not exactly the cheeriest advice, but hey, lots of people don't have ten good days in their entire lives. If you make a point of it, the odds are you can be happier than most people inside the first month."

"Hmm." It didn't sound like he was buying it.

"It's possible Earth might outlast us. The Kalirae have been around for centuries." David looked out his side window at the outer ring. "And who knows, we might be able to outlast the Earth. We've got spaceships, and the planets are close enough together here that we could shuttle whole populations from place to place if things get too bad in one spot. If we can learn to cooperate with the aliens, this could turn out all right. A lot more interesting than our old solar system, anyway."

"May you live in interesting times," Rick said softly.

"What?"

"An old curse. I always thought it was kind of dumb. I mean, don't people *want* an exciting life? But now I think I know what it means. I want concerts and movies and trips around the world. I don't want a war with the Soviets and spatial anomalies and trips *through* the world."

David couldn't help the silly grin that spread across his face. They had actually gone straight through the planet. "It'll make a great story to tell your grandkids."

"Grandkids? Are you serious? What's the point in bringing up grandkids if this is all they have to look forward to?"

"People have been saying that since the dawn of time," David said. "Everybody thinks their time is the worst there ever was. When you're a teenager life hardly seems worth living, and then when you get older you get a job and house payments. The next batch of teenagers listens to crappy music and the generation ahead of you flies too slow. People somehow still manage to have babies."

Raedawn came up the steps again and stood in the doorway. "What are you babbling about?"

"Just trying to spread a little cheer."

"Talking about babies? Get real."

"He's already got one."

"Oh." She waved her right hand toward the back of the ship. "I had to seal off one of the missile-loading ports. Whatever we hit whacked the door."

"Which one?" Rick asked.

"Number three."

He poked at his tactical screen, locking that missile out of the firing order. "No telling how bad the one in the tube is damaged. I'd hate to have it blow prematurely if we tried to launch it. Might screw up our whole day."

"Right," she said. "It was going so well." She squeezed past him into her seat again. "So what's the plan?"

David shrugged. "Go home. Get court-martialed. Rot in prison. Maybe learn to draw."

"Hmm. Dreamer." She looked at Earth, still receding even though the engines were laboring at full power to reduce their outward velocity. Then she craned her head forward and looked from side to side. "Where'd the anomaly go?"

"Back where laps go when you stand up," said David. "We're stuck here now."

She bit her lower lip. "That explains the talk about babies. Men always want to procreate at the strangest times."

Rick snorted, then burst into a coughing fit.

"Don't blow a lung, there, soldier," she said.

"Sorry," he said when he got it under control again. "Caught me by surprise."

"After what we just went through, I don't think anything could surprise me," Raedawn grumbled.

David saw a flicker of motion out the window. When he looked up to see what it was, he nearly leaped out of his seat. Four sleek, silvery spacecraft had just flashed past them on a course for Earth. They looked familiar, with three large fins in back and wedge-shaped noses with tiny cockpits a third of the way back, but it took him a second to realize where he'd seen a ship like that before. They weren't Union ships, nor Neo-Sov, nor did they belong to any other nation on Earth.

He turned to Raedawn. "You, uh, were expecting a Kalirae fleet?"

23

hat the hell are they doing here?" Raedawn asked. "And why now?"

David aimed the telescope dead ahead and tried to catch the ships amid the cloudscape of Earth. "I'd guess they want to catch us with our pants down."

Rick said, "Four ships isn't exactly a fleet, unless they're a lot more technologically advanced than we are."

"We hit one with a missile," Raedawn pointed out. "They're not invincible."

He looked at their receding images in the 'scope screen. "They must know that. Are they asking for permission to land?"

David switched on the radio again and began scanning through the standard comm channels, but there was so much traffic it was impossible to tell if the Kalirae were transmitting as well. As he listened to situation reports and calls for assistance, he realized Earth and Luna were in total panic over what had just happened. The Soviets were blaming the Union for it, and the Union was blaming the Soviets.

"That's not right," he said when he heard that last accusation. "The least they could do is have the decency to blame us." He switched on the transmitter and ran the power all the way up, then said, "That's a total load of crap! *Nyet,* false, bullshitski! I'm the person responsible for what just happened. David Hutchins, acting completely on my own. I brought the spatial anomaly back to Earth, and I take full responsibility for that, but the responsibility for failing to use it properly falls directly on all of you. You were supposed to blow it open when it got there! If you'd done that, we'd have all gone back to where we came from, and we'd all be celebrating now instead of bickering about whose fault it is."

People heard him, that much was clear, but the response from hundreds of transmitters on the same frequency overwhelmed the signal processors' ability to sort them out. All that came through was a babble of voices filled with static.

Closer at hand, though, the reception was crystal clear. "Thanks a lot, idiot," said Raedawn. "You just blew any chance we might have had of fading into the woodwork."

"We had no chance of that anyway. We're screwed." He looked out at Earth again, then back inside. "Rick might not be. He did try to stop us. If we testify to that, he could—"

"Something's happening up ahead." Rick pointed at the telescope screen, where one of the Kalirae ships had reversed course and was coming back toward them.

"Oh shit," David said. "They heard our transmission, too."

"How could they tell what you said?" Raedawn asked.

"I don't know, but get ready to fight if they shoot at us."

Rick double-checked his tactical display. "It's just one ship. That's a hopeful sign."

Then the radio boomed with a signal strong enough to override all the others. "David Hutchins. Do you hear?" The accent was foreign. Not just unusual; this was unearthly.

Deep and gravelly, filled with overtones from nonhuman vocal cords. There could be no doubt where it came from.

"I hear you." He turned down the outgoing power so he wouldn't be broadcasting all the way to Earth, and he lowered the volume so the aliens' response wouldn't blast them out of the cockpit again. The background chatter faded to a whisper as well.

"We have come for Harxae."

"He's on Earth. He didn't come with us this time."

"We know. You will help us . . . rescue him." Their words came slowly, as if they were unfamiliar with them even though they knew what to say.

"What's wrong? Is he in trouble? Are you in contact with him?"

"He is held . . . captive. Yes, we are."

So Harxae's telepathy worked over interplanetary distance, at least with his own kind. These newcomers were too far away to pick the words they needed out of David's mind, so they had to be getting them from Harxae, who must be riffling through his guards' minds and relaying the concepts outward. They wouldn't need that for long, though. The Kalirae ship was accelerating hard. Combined with the Union ship's deceleration, they would rendezvous within minutes.

David didn't like the news that Harxae was being held captive. Or was he? "He was in a hospital when we left, recovering from a leg wound. He wasn't actually a prisoner."

"He is a prisoner," came the eerie voice.

David was puzzled. Was Harxae officially a prisoner or were the Kalirae misunderstanding? "Have you tried just asking the Union to let you take him back?"

There was a short silence as they puzzled out what he had said. "No. Would they do that?"

"It's worth a try before you go in with guns and . . . those talismans."

"We would lose the element of surprise."

David snorted. "He's on a military base. Surprise isn't going to do you much good anyway. Not unless you want to fight a major war."

"We just want to rescue our own."

David could feel the growing possibility that something really bad might transpire here. He thought through the options. "Try asking politely. If that doesn't work, threaten politely. That should do the trick. I don't think the Union wants to fight a war on two fronts."

"We do not fight wars."

"No? What do you do with all those weapons you guys carry?"

They apparently had to dig a while for the right word, but when it finally came, there was no ambiguity: "We exterminate."

"Lovely," Raedawn whispered. Her expression left no doubt what she thought of this whole situation and of David's part in it. It was like last night had never happened.

"What, uh, what are your intentions with us?" he asked, not taking his eyes from her as he spoke.

"You will help us," the Kalira said again. It wasn't a request.

"I'll do what I can. Ask Harxae if Lamott's there."

"He is not."

"All right. He's probably off fighting brush fires somewhere else. Uh . . . that's a figure of speech. But we've got a little time, so let's wait until you get within mind-reading range of me before we try to talk to him. You should do the talking, but you'll be able to draw on my knowledge of English and what I know about him as well. With any luck we can come to an agreement that doesn't involve . . . exterminating anybody."

"Agreed."

David switched off the transmitter, leaving the receiver on in case the Kalira had more to say.

"What do you think?" he asked.

"I think we're in deep shit," said Raedawn. "I don't think this guy's in the mood to negotiate."

Rick nodded his head. "But if we help them and they turn hostile, then we'll be collaborating with the enemy."

"I'm trying to keep them from becoming the enemy," David said.

Raedawn still glared at him. "If you'd kept your stupid mouth shut, we wouldn't have the spotlight on us right now."

"If I'd kept my mouth shut, the Union would have escalated their attack on the Neo-Soviet empire. As it was, I took away their excuse."

"As if they need one."

"Yeah, so they'll continue to fight, but they won't be able to blame it on me."

Rick looked distinctly uncomfortable to be sitting between the two of them. Even so, he said, "Um, sir? They didn't want to blame it on you. They wanted to blame it on each other."

"Don't you start picking nits, too."

Raedawn didn't give him a chance to respond. " 'Too'? Is that what I'm doing, picking nits? Well, let's cut right to the—"

"Sirs? Shouldn't we be getting ready for the rendezvous?"

Raedawn glowered at him, but he held his ground.

"They've turned over and are decelerating to match our velocity."

The alien ship's drive flame was visible by naked eye now and growing brighter as they watched.

"Should we cut our own deceleration?" David asked.

"Never change your course when someone's trying to rendezvous," Raedawn said. "Besides, at fifteen gees they won't be able to board us unless we actually dock with them, and we can prevent that just by varying our thrust a little."

"Good point."

If that mollified her, she gave no outward sign. He sighed. Why had he ever thought she would be any different now? She was the same person today that she had been yesterday, and so was he. They had shared something new, but it hadn't changed who they were.

The Kalirae ship bore down on them, but they still had a couple of minutes before it arrived. "It's probably pointless with them," David said, "but let me get us some hand weapons to keep up here with us just in case."

He got up and went into the back, remembering the gravity shift on the stairway just in time to keep from tripping when he hit the Earth-normal field in the cargo hold. The space was mostly empty now, since they had fired all the EMP missiles. It echoed as he opened the weapons locker beside the airlock and removed three hand pistols from their clips, then shut the door and climbed the stairs again.

"Here," he said, handing one each to Raedawn and Rick. "If we get close enough to need these, we're probably already dead, but you never know."

Rick took his pistol and examined its power and lockout settings. Satisfied that it would fire when he needed it, he stuck it to the tear-away patch on the left side of his belt so he could cross-draw it. David looked to his own belt and realized he had the same arrangement, thanks to the borrowed uniform, so he stuck his pistol in the same place. Raedawn had no military belt, but she had plenty of pockets in her black leather jacket. She unzipped one on the right side and stuck her pistol into it, where it made another breast-sized lump below her natural one.

They watched the Kalirae ship approach and match their velocity, then move closer with small bursts from its thrusters. It was huge, at least ten times bigger than Harxae's and Gavwin's ship even though it followed the same basic design. The fins in back were big enough to live in, and the cockpit-shaped bubble covered an operations center big enough to play volleyball under. Tiny shapes moving about inside had to be the crew. David counted at least a dozen of them, all tall and willowy, all green or blue-green.

The radio continued to natter with the faint background chatter of Earth message traffic, then the rich voice of the Kalira came back on. "We are within range. Let us now communicate our demands to your superior." Now that it could read David's mind, the alien's labored pronunciation was gone, as was most of the odd harmonic to its voice.

He turned on the transmitter again. "We're asking, not demanding, at least at first."

"Understood."

"Don't threaten first, and don't threaten at all if you can help it."

"This course of action is foreign to us, but your minds reveal no deception." There was a moment of silence, then the alien added, "Even though you are not agreed among yourselves that this is the right thing to do."

David looked to the others. "What else should we do?"

The Kalira answered before either of them could. "Get him out ourselves and leave you alone. Abandon him and leave Earth alone."

David knew which thoughts were whose. He said, "I see. How do you feel about those two options?"

"They suck." The alien made a smacking sound. "What an interesting phrase. An interesting image as well. No, we will not abandon him, though we fully intend to get him out ourselves if your assistance does not serve. We stand ready to make the attempt. I can read your thoughts well enough to choose the words I need. Shall we commence?"

"Go for it."

"You may wish to reduce the gain on your receiver."

David turned it down a notch. He'd been transmitting at low gain so he wouldn't interfere with Earth traffic; now the background noise faded to a gentle hiss as he turned down the incoming signal as well.

"More."

It creeped him out that the Kalira seemed to see what he was doing through his own eyes, but he turned the volume down some more. "What are you going to do?"

"Shout," said the now barely audible voice. David resisted the urge to turn it up again, and a moment later he was glad he had. The alien voice, once again full of harmonics and deep as the bottom of a well, said, "Quiet down there!"

"That was tactful," Raedawn said.

"Since when did you care about tact?" David asked, but she had no time to respond even if she wanted to. Verbally, anyway. Her nonverbal response said enough.

The Kalirae voice boomed over the radio again, still alien but much more understandable now. "This is Kalirae patrol. We wish to talk with General Perry Lamott of Union Space Command in Great Falls, Montana. Speak to us."

If there was a response, it was too faint to hear.

"Speeeak to us!"

David risked turning up the volume for a second, then snapped it back down when he heard nothing.

"It'll take them a minute to roust him," he said.

"Your system is cumbersome," said the alien. "Why invent radio if you cannot reach one another instantly with it?" His voice was much softer now; apparently he was transmitting just ship-to-ship. David had to turn up the radio so they could hear him clearly.

He supposed a telepathic society might feel that way about instant access. Hell, he'd felt that way himself when he was back on Mars with a communicator clapped to his ear half the time, but he suddenly realized how glad he was to be rid of that. There were times when a person didn't want to be disturbed.

"I see," said the alien. "Interesting concept. It may amuse you to know that you all agree."

Raedawn looked at David, puzzlement mixing with annoyance in her expression.

"We've got no secrets with these guys around," he said.

"Apparently not."

The radio crackled, and a tiny voice said, "Kalirae patrol, please hold for General Lamott."

"We wait." David scrambled for the volume control again.

A few seconds later, Lamott himself said, "This is General Lamott."

The alien made himself a bit more understandable, and didn't shout. David turned the volume down about midway while he said, "You have one of our people. We have come to take him home."

"I see. We had hoped to have a chance to talk with him first."

"You have had your chance, but were afraid to take it. Opportunity has gone to another door."

"Your kind aren't familiar to us," Lamott said. "We proceeded cautiously. But we would like to establish diplomatic relations."

"You are new to the Maelstrom, so I will not laugh, but do not expect diplomacy to get results here."

"Give us a chance," said Lamott. "Like you said, we're new here. We need to learn how things work."

"Another time," said the Kalira. "Harxae is injured. He is our first priority."

"We're taking good care of him. You'd be welcome to make sure, of course. But please stay. And be our guests, of course."

"We cannot."

Other voices buzzed in the background, then Lamott said, "Then at least let some of us go with you."

Raedawn shot David a look of consternation. "What the hell is going on down there?"

The alien's voice became softer again as he transmitted ship-to-ship. "What is his intent?"

David turned up the gain, including Raedawn in his reply. "To learn more about you. Humans are curious. We've never met aliens before."

"I see." Loudly, he said. "We agree. We will allow David Hutchins to travel with us."

Everyone on the ship started with surprise.

"What!" Lamott practically shouted over the radio. "Not him. He's a loose cannon. He damned near got us all killed just a few minutes ago. He cannot represent humanity."

"We are interested in him for his mind."

Raedawn laughed. "That's what they all say."

Lamott continued. "We can't allow David to represent humanity," he said. "Anybody but him."

"Very well. Raedawn Corona."

She sat forward. "Hey, I didn't say I wanted to go."

"You didn't need to," said David, tapping his forehead with his finger.

"Dammit, I don't *want* to."

"Really?"

She sat back. "At least I don't think I do."

"Do you wish to know?" asked the Kalira.

"No! Stay out of my head!"

"That is impossible."

Lamott couldn't hear the low-power conversation between ships. Surprisingly, he said, "That's acceptable. But we want Hutchins here."

"Where he goes is his own choice," the Kalira said.

Lamott must have realized he was fighting a losing battle. "You've also got one of our soldiers out there. We want him back."

"He wants to return," said the Kalira. "That is acceptable."

"Understood. We'll, uh, we'll be waiting for you. Lamott out."

David let out a long sigh. "And you said diplomacy wouldn't get results."

24

They landed in the spaceport just as the Tkona was setting behind the western hills. The Kalirae ship touched down right beside the Union ship, looming over it like a hawk over a sparrow. The other three ships had never rendezvoused with them. David had no idea what had become of them, and didn't ask. One alien ship that size on Earth at a time was enough.

Lamott was waiting for them when they stepped out of the airlock, with a dozen armed soldiers backing him up, their weapons held ready. He had apparently decided the risk of revealing state secrets was worth the chance to meet with humanity's new neighbors. Either that or he had been ordered to do so.

Lamott obviously didn't think there was any point in hiding his thoughts anymore. When the airlock door opened and he saw David standing at the top of the ramp, he said, "Well, there's the happy traitor home from the hunt. How's it feel to throw in with aliens against your own species?"

"How's it feel to doom the entire world to eternity in chaos?" David retorted. "You fucking idiot! Why didn't you blow up the nebula and send Earth home when you had the chance?"

"Because it wasn't home," Lamott said smugly.

"What?"

"We analyzed the video from your shuttle. When the Kalirae missile blew apart your little gateway, the star pattern you saw didn't match anything familiar."

He couldn't have hit David any harder with his fist. Not familiar? He had been so sure the gateway led back home again. How could it not? It had come from there. It had a solar radiation spectrum. Where else could those momentary glimpses of normal space have come from?

"Turns out it wasn't even a star pattern," Lamott went on. "As near as we can figure, what you saw was this same disk of planets and debris that we're stuck in, just from another angle."

If that was true, it meant that everything else David knew about the anomaly could be wrong. He felt his knees buckle slightly and a wave of nausea came over him. How could that be?

Lamott tossed him a bone. "One thing worked right: the extra mountain range that appeared over by Missoula during the Change vanished just as mysteriously when we went through the anomaly again."

David was still unable to speak. He had moved a mountain. Ordinarily that would have impressed the hell out of him, but he had expected to move a planet. It was apparently a good thing he hadn't, but the magnitude of his failure was moving mountains inside of him. He was reeling with the inner shift required for him to process this information.

He had no time to recover before the Kalirae ship's airlock tilted out to become a ramp and a bright-green-skinned alien stepped down it. He carried a long staff with a fist-sized opening at one end. The air seemed to shimmer around him, but it could have been just a trick of the evening shadows.

"Welcome to Earth," Lamott said. "I'm General Lamott. But then, you probably already know that, don't you?"

"Welcome to the Maelstrom," the Kalira replied. He tilted his oblong head, then said, "I am Navrel, and I know many things about you. Some of them pleasant."

Navrel stared at Lamott. "Harxae is not here. You think to delay my departure by needlessly insisting that I see him in your hospital. Very well." The shimmering air around him expanded and grew darker, then he suddenly vanished.

"What the hell? Where'd he go?" demanded Lamott. "You didn't tell me they could do that!"

"I didn't know they could," said David.

Lamott whirled around and yelled at the soldiers, "Split up! Find him!" but before they could move, the air swirled again, the darkness returned, and Navrel stood before them once more—with Harxae beside him. Harxae's leg was still wrapped in its bandage, but he supported his own weight while Navrel held what David thought must be some sort of weapon. For a second nobody moved, then Navrel slowly relaxed.

"Time to go," Navrel said to Raedawn.

"What? We just got here! If I'm going to leave with you for who knows how long, I'd like to pack some things."

"We can make you anything you need."

"Brassieres? Pants? Extra shirts? No offense, but it doesn't look like clothing is high on you guys' list of priorities. And how about toothbrushes?"

"We can make anything you need," Navrel said again. "We must go now."

She ran a hand through her hair. "At least let me get my bag off the ship. It's right here."

"Go, then, but hurry."

David followed her up the ramp. "I'm going, too."

"I figured you were."

"Is that okay with you?" He didn't mean the question to sound belligerent, but the stress in his voice made it come out wrong.

"Do what you like. I'm sure there's room enough for us to avoid each other if we—"

"Stop."

She did, halfway up the stairs to the upper deck. "Now what?"

"Just stop being so touchy for a minute. I don't give a rip about the Kalirae. I mean, it's great to meet aliens and all that, but I want to go with *you*." He swallowed, then said, as softly as he could manage, "Okay?"

She leaned back against the railing. "I thought guys were supposed to get all cold and distant after a night in the sack."

"Surprise."

"Well, I'll be damned. You mean I've been bitchy and defensive all day for nothing?"

"You haven't been bitchy all day." He grinned weakly. "Just most of it."

She rolled her eyes and took a step down toward him, but he never learned what she intended to do because just then the sound of gunfire erupted from outside.

"Shit!" He whirled around and rushed for the airlock, but a hail of bullets bouncing off the ceiling convinced him that was a bad idea. He dropped to the floor, yelled, "Get down!" and pulled his pistol from his belt.

She yelped and clattered down the stairs, sprawling beside him and clawing at her chest. At first he thought she was going for her own gun, then he saw the bright red stain against the black leather.

"No!" he screamed. He fired his pistol wildly out the door, then jumped up and slapped the emergency close button halfway up the left side. The airlock slammed shut with enough force to rattle his teeth, cutting off the bullets from outside. He could still hear them bouncing off the hull, but he bent down next to Raedawn, who was holding her left hand tight against the right side of her chest.

"How bad is it?" he asked.

"I don't . . . think I want to know." She was breathing hard, and her whole body shook from the pain. Blood flowed around her fingers.

"Hang tight," he said, standing up and slapping his pistol back onto his belt. "I'm going to get you to the hospital."

"How?"

"We're in a spaceship."

"You can't . . . land there."

"They've got a parking lot."

"Jesus, David. It's . . . full of cars."

"And you've got a bullet hole in your chest!"

He turned and took the stairs two at a time, nearly hitting his head on the ceiling when he hit Martian gravity on the upper deck. He jumped into the left-hand chair and switched on the agravs, then ran the throttle forward until the ship leaped into the air. He immediately cut the power and let it arc over so he could see the base. He recognized the hoverpath they had taken before and followed it with his eyes until he spotted the boxy medical building. The emergency vehicle pad on the roof confirmed that it was the right one, but the ship was way too big to land there. It would crush the whole building.

He looked for the main ground entrance, then brought the ship down in front of it, pausing only long enough to let anyone below flee the area before he dropped it the last dozen meters onto the ground. He felt trees snap and cars buckle beneath its bulk, then the ship bumped hard and stayed put. He switched off the agravs and rushed down the stairs again, slapped the door button, and turned to Raedawn.

"This is probably going to hurt," he said as he bent down to scoop her up in his arms.

"It already does," she whispered.

"Here goes."

He slid his hands underneath her and picked her up. She kept her left hand tight against her chest, but she put her right arm around his neck as he rushed outside and down the ramp, staggering under her weight in the full Earth gravity.

"My hero," she whispered as she leaned her head against his chest.

"Hang on. We're almost there."

The automatic doors didn't open fast enough. He kicked them out of the way and rushed on in, stumbling up to the admissions desk, where he deposited her on the counter with his last ounce of strength. "Gunshot," he told the startled ward clerk, a middle-aged woman who had just been getting up to see what all the commotion was outside. "She's been hit!"

The clerk took one look at Raedawn and immediately forgot the spaceship in her parking lot. She snatched up her phone and said, "Code blue to the admissions desk. Code blue, gunshot."

Footsteps pounded down the corridor behind her, and two orderlies in soft green scrubs rushed in, saw Raedawn lying on the counter, and grabbed one of the gurneys waiting in the hallway. David helped them move her onto it, then followed them down the corridor to the emergency room.

"Sir, you can't go in there!" the ward clerk protested, but he ignored her and she apparently considered her duty filled with one warning.

The orderlies rushed out and a doctor rushed in, still tying on a surgical apron, then he gently lifted Raedawn's hand, pulled her jacket aside, and pressed a bandage into the wound without removing her shirt. The hole was well to the right of center, just under her breast, and it gurgled as she breathed.

"You're going to be okay," David told her. "You're going to be okay. Isn't she?"

The doctor whistled softly. "That's a nasty wound, but yes, I think she'll live." He turned toward the cabinet beside the door for another bandage, but he stopped in midmotion. The air swirled, a patch of blackness formed, and Navrel stood there before him.

The Kalira took in the entire situation in one glance, then said, "How quaint." He stepped up to Raedawn and held his hands over her, then the air shimmered and they both were gone.

The doctor opened and closed his mouth a few times, then said, "What was that?"

"Somebody who'd damn well better know what he's doing, or I'm going to put a bullet hole in *him*."

He got his chance a moment later when the Kalira rematerialized beside him. "She's hurt, dammit!" David said. "She needs help before you snatch her off—"

There was a moment of discontinuity, then they stood in a different emergency room, this one larger, with three other Kalirae standing over Raedawn, who lay on an exam table twice as long as it needed to be. The aliens weren't touching her, though. They held their arms extended over her like Navrel had, but from their hands a soft blue-green light began to descend, wrapping itself around her upper body like a cocoon.

Raedawn gasped, then stopped breathing.

"Navrel!" David growled, pulling his gun from his belt.

"She lives. See." Navrel's eyes never left Raedawn. David looked at her again, saw her chest rise and fall, saw her eyelids flutter, and put his pistol away.

"Our methods are faster," Navrel said. He nodded to the exam table beside her, where Harxae rested, the bandage removed from his thigh and the bullet hole nowhere in evidence.

"It seemed expedient to leave before someone else got hurt," Navrel said.

"What happened?" David asked. "Who started shooting?"

"One of the soldiers," said the Kalira. "I knew he was xenophobic, but I misjudged the extent of his fear. When Harxae stumbled going up the ramp he thought we were about to attack, so he fired on us. In the confusion that followed, everyone else opened fire as well."

"Did you . . . did you hurt them?"

"That was not necessary."

He was surprised to find that he actually cared, even about Lamott. Then Raedawn sat up and he rushed forward, all thoughts of Lamott forgotten.

"Are you all right?" He reached out for her, but didn't know where to touch. She was like some delicate crystal sculpture that had miraculously escaped an earthquake, and now he was afraid to risk going near.

"That was . . . bizarre," she said. She raised her arms experimentally, then twisted her chest from side to side. The

bloodstained shirt and jacket glistened in the bright overhead light, but she showed no evidence of pain. The three
Kalirae who had healed her bowed slightly, then turned
away.

"Hey!" she said.

As one, they turned back toward her.

"Thanks."

They bowed again, then left the room.

"Vow of silence?" she asked Navrel.

Navrel gave a little shrug of his bony shoulders. "There
was understanding enough without words."

She reached out for David, and he helped her off the
exam table. Gravity here was somewhere between Earth and
Mars normal.

He hugged her, gently at first, then tighter when she
didn't cry out. He kissed her, and she seemed to be okay
with that, too, but a moment later she backed away and said,
"Oh, yuck."

"Yuck?"

"I got blood all over you."

His uniform had a big stain just below the left pocket.
He felt a brief moment of panic at the sight of so much
blood, still fresh and red, but he fought it down. She was
okay. He pulled her close and kissed her again.

"That's all right," he said. "This time. Just don't do it
again."

25

here are we now?" Raedawn asked.

Navrel tilted his head as if listening to a distant voice. "In space. We are currently engaged in battle. Come see." He said it nonchalantly, as if space battles were a natural part of any trip.

They weren't natural for David, even though he'd been in more than his share lately. He felt the skin crawl on the back of his neck at the thought that missiles might be approaching at that very moment. "The Union is still trying to shoot us down?"

"No. I believe the first wave were Pharons. Others have since joined them. The Shard are standing off to let us wear each other down. Come."

Raedawn took a cloth from the side of the exam table and wiped off the worst of the blood from her shirt and jacket, then she and David followed Navrel and Harxae through the ship to the control room.

It felt like they were in an office building: wide corridors with high ceilings, rooms opening off to either side, elevators and stairways for moving between levels. Even though the ship must be maneuvering, there was no sense of motion. Kalirae engines and artificial gravity generators were apparently more tightly attuned to one another than human ones.

"Other races?" David asked as they walked. "What's going on? Did they all decide to gang up on Earth, or are they after you?"

"Considering how quickly they arrived, I believe they were already coming simply to investigate the latest arrival in the Maelstrom," Navrel told him, "but now they're after *you*."

"Me?"

"Yes. They don't know it's you in particular whom they seek, but they all watched an Earth spaceship approach the remnant of the veil that brought your world here, and they watched you manipulate it and lead it where you wished. They watched holes appear in it, however briefly. You did something no one has seen before, and they all want to find out how you did it."

"Me," David said again.

"Yes. They chase us because it's clear that we got to you first."

Raedawn, holding his hand as they walked side by side through the immense ship, gave him an odd little smile. "Sounds like you're almost as hot an item as you think you are."

"He doesn't regard himself as— Oh. I see. That was sarcasm."

They turned a corner, and Navrel led them down another corridor. Raedawn eyed him speculatively. "You wouldn't by any chance be after the same thing everybody else is, would you? That was what's called a rhetorical question, in case you were wondering."

His wrinkled face grew even more so. "Yes, we are also

interested in learning what he knows. Perhaps our combined knowledge will prove useful, since we do know a little about the Maelstrom ourselves." He paused, then added, "That was what's called an understatement."

"First things first," said David. "How do we get past those alien ships, and what can they do to Earth if we don't stop them?"

Navrel gave him a puzzled look. "We fight our way past them, of course. And what they do to Earth is not our concern."

"It is *mine*. I'm not going to stand back and let them attack my homeworld because of something I did."

"You are not in a position to do anything else."

"No? I think maybe I am. You can take what I know out of my brain, but you can't take how I think. If I refuse to work with you, my knowledge isn't worth a tenth of what it could be." In fact, he thought, if Lamott was right, then it wasn't worth a damned thing.

The Kalira bit his lip in a decidedly human gesture. He looked at Harxae, who looked back, their eyes locking in intense concentration. Were they trying to hypnotize each other into agreement? David had no idea how deep a level their conversation occurred on, but it only took a few seconds before they broke it off and Navrel said, "What do you propose? We are only four ships against many."

Four ships the size of battle cruisers, David thought, but he hadn't seen what they were up against. Fortunately, he didn't intend to fight them all if he didn't have to. "Who's faster, us or them?" he asked.

"We are, but not by a wide margin."

"So much the better. They wouldn't chase us unless they thought they stood a chance of catching us."

"Do we want them to chase us?" Raedawn asked.

"Just long enough to draw them away from Earth," he said. "And to pick each other off when they think they've got the upper hand."

They approached a wide door at the end of the corridor. It slid sideways into the wall when they drew close, revealing the inside of the vast domed control room. Ten to fifteen Kalirae stood at their stations, flying, shooting, and communicating with the other ships in perfect coordination and total silence.

"Yes," Navrel said in answer to his unvoiced thought. "We can be of one mind when we wish it."

The dome was clear as glass. It looked as if they were standing on the outer hull while the battle raged overhead. Bright flashes appeared in space, the white, symmetrical ones indicating near misses; the reddish, ragged ones revealing hits. Drive flames drew arcs through the darkness.

"Holy . . . how many ships?" whispered Raedawn.

"Forty-three," said Navrel. There was another red blast. "Forty-two."

"Ten to one," said David. "Not the best of odds, but they'll have to do. At least they're fighting among themselves, as well as with us."

He tried to spot concentrations of ships. There were three obvious alliances, each taking occasional pot shots at one another as they poured most of their firepower at their mutual objective. David couldn't see the other three Kalirae ships, but he could tell where they were by the continual barrage of antimissile fire spreading out from three separate points in space beside and behind their own. The defense seemed sufficient; nothing got even close. It looked like the Kalirae strategy was to wear down their attackers' numbers through attrition, but the Kalirae ships would have to take an ungodly amount of incoming fire to do that. No matter how good their defenses, something was bound to slip through eventually.

And Earth, hanging like a glass Christmas ornament behind them, was way too close for comfort.

"Let's make a break for it," David said.

"We are not in a good position for that," Navrel protested.

"Then they won't be expecting it, will they? That's the best time. Make like we're going to attack, fire a few missiles to keep 'em busy, then split up and go like hell for deep space."

Navrel didn't have to relay the command. The other Kalirae in the control room picked up on David's thoughts, reached consensus, and acted before words would have become necessary.

The immense craft leaped toward one of the three clusters of alien ships. David smiled as he realized that he was already thinking of the Kalirae ship as his own. Only the unknown enemies were "alien." They scattered when the Kalirae fired on them, but regrouped immediately and poured a steady barrage of missiles at the fleeing ship.

Off in the distance, two other Kalirae ships each drew their own retinue in their wake. The fourth joined one of the others, the one with the biggest following. Earth fell behind, ignored in the heat of the chase.

"Okay, now we cross paths. Force the clusters of ships behind us to pass right through each other."

That plan needed no relaying, either, not even to the other ships. The Kalirae craft angled toward one another, crossed close enough to make David and Raedawn cling together in surprise, then split apart again.

David watched behind them. The pursuing ships might as well have gone through a shredder. Half their number erupted in spectacular explosions, the first few taken out by missiles and the rest by their debris. The survivors were the ones who went wide at the first sign of trouble, but they regrouped again, and this time there was no more firing between them.

"Plan B," said David. "Do you have—?"

He didn't need to finish his thought. Even as he was voicing it, the Kalirae ships each vented thousands of gallons of water from their holding tanks. It immediately flashed to vapor in the vacuum of space, but it had the same mass either way. The pursuing ships veered frantically aside, but five more didn't make it in time. At the speed they were going, even water vapor hit like a brick wall, smashing open their hulls and spilling their contents into space.

There were maybe fifteen ships left. These stayed well away from each other as their commanders reconsidered their positions and their strategy.

"Okay," David said. "Let's look for fast space and run for it."

"Fast space?" Raedawn asked.

David tapped his watch. "Pi equals two or less." He set it into calculator mode and called up the constant, but space was actually flatter here than usual: 3.37 and rising.

"Have you got a better way of finding tightly curved space than I do?" he asked.

Harxae said, "Yes, I can sense it." He stepped away from the others, held his arms out wide, and turned around like a radar antenna. "There," he said, pointing upward and to their right. "It is not strong, but it is faster than where we are."

"All right. All four of us should angle toward it, then drop more water so the ships behind us have to go around."

"An old strategy, but a good one," Navrel said.

The ships drew closer, and David kept checking the value of pi until it bottomed out at 2.5. "This looks like it," he said, just as Harxae said, "We have reached the heart of it."

The ship beside them vented another water tank, but needn't have bothered. None of the pursuers had even attempted to follow directly behind them this time.

The faster space gave them half again as much lead as they had before. Harxae did his radar trick twice more, and the distance increased each time. After that they were far enough ahead that the other ships could see the vapor clouds coming and dodge, then tuck back in and use the same fast space to keep up.

"What's ahead of us?" Raedawn asked. "Any friendly planets we can loop past for some cover fire?"

"There are no friendly planets," Navrel said.

"Not even your homeworld?"

"We will not take our problems there. They have battles enough to fight without us bringing more."

David had never let go of Raedawn's hand. He liked the feel of it in his. "It's hard to believe nobody makes alliances here," he said. "It just doesn't make sense."

"Situations change too quickly," said Navrel. "A strong planet today could be rubble tomorrow. No one wants to be allied with refugees."

"That's a pretty harsh attitude."

"This is a harsh place." Navrel pointed back toward the pursuing ships. "Look. More have joined the chase. These may not even know what the others are after, but they know it must be valuable so they come to investigate. They will attract even more."

"Then we've got to shake them once and for all."

Navrel shook his head, a human gesture no doubt borrowed just for his human audience. "We should have fought our way through when it was just the curious. They only suspected that we had something they want, but by running, we proved it. They will not shake easily."

"How about that instant-elsewhere thing you did back on Earth? Can you do that with the whole ship?"

"That would require the power of our entire population. Neither we nor the ship would survive the attempt."

"Well, we've got to do something," David said. "If this goes on much longer, everybody with a spaceship is going to be on our tails."

"Agreed," Navrel said. "Have you another brilliant Earth strategy?"

"I don't know. Do I?" David was at a loss for more ideas, but there must be tons of them rattling around inside his head.

Navrel focused on him as if looking through his skull into his thoughts, then said, "You have a bloody history. The Trojan horse is an interesting idea, but I don't see how it would work for us here. Pongee sticks are equally diabolical, but equally useless in space. The same goes for ambush, sniper fire, poison, terrorism, blitzkrieg, siege, and playing bad music at high volume."

"You're looking for attack strategies," Raedawn said. "But we're trying to get away."

"That is a foreign concept. Perhaps I simply don't recognize the solution when I see it."

She said, "You should look into *my* head if you want foreign. Spies don't fight unless they have to. We go to ground, or disguise ourselves, or strike a deal, or—"

"Or fund guerrillas, or spread rumors, or rig elections to destabilize governments. Yes, I see. None of which will work here."

"How about giving up?" she said.

David had been looking out at the pursuing ships. He snapped his head back toward her again. "Give up? What?"

"It's the oldest trick in the book. When they've got you surrounded, surrender. But swallow the data, and give them a useless chip with a code that'll take 'em weeks to decipher. Then when they put you in the cell full of snakes, toss one at the guard who brings your food, take his gun when he panics, and make your escape. Of course you sabotage the power plant and blow up the bad guys' headquarters on your way out, but that's just for fun."

She was grinning by the time she reached the end of her "idea."

"You forgot the part about seducing the sexy henchman," he said.

"We save that trick for emergencies. Along with suicide pills and jumping out of a moving train from a bridge over a river."

He squeezed her hand, then looked up at Navrel. "Okay, so we're fresh out of ideas. What do you suggest?"

"You just said it," the Kalira said. "Giving up. Suicide pills. And jumping out of a moving train. Together, it just might work."

26

ou want to take the ship *where*?" David asked.

They had gone to an observation alcove at the front edge of the control room, where they took in a nearly unobstructed view of the entire pocket universe while Navrel outlined his plan.

He said, "To the edge of the Tkona. The vortex at the center of the Maelstrom."

"I know what the Tkona is. From Harxae's description of it, it sounds like a good place to stay away from."

"Precisely. We will lose most of our pursuit when they realize where we intend to go."

"But not everyone."

"That depends on how closely we approach it. If we accelerate straight toward it, it will look as if we intend to sacrifice ourselves rather than let the enemy have our secret. But to do that, we must pass through areas so dense with energy whorls that sensors will be useless. Nontelepathic races will have no way to navigate there, but we can keep our ships far enough apart that we can watch out for one another. We should be able to shake our pursuit there."

"And if not?"

"Then we will attempt the 'instant elsewhere trick' as you call it. But we will do it your way instead of ours."

"My way requires a spatial anomaly like the one that brought us here," David reminded him. "And from what Lamott told me, it doesn't actually take you anywhere anyway."

"The Tkona is anomaly enough for our purposes. And even if we cannot escape the Maelstrom, using it as a temporary route to someplace else within it would allow us to shake our pursuit and study your discovery at the same time."

"My discovery isn't really much of a discovery," David said. "You can attract an existing anomaly and manipulate its shape with magnets, and you can blow one open with bombs. If you're in the right place at the right time, you can open up where there wasn't one before. That's all I know."

"That's more than we knew before. We knew how to open a gateway with our minds and how to direct where it takes us, but only to another point within the Maelstrom, and we were never able to duplicate the effect mechanically." Navrel looked out at the vortex in the distance. "Your way seems to allow the same kind of thing on a larger scale. We will not try it this time, but if we can move instantly through the Tkona without detection, it will look as if we were swallowed up."

It would be so much simpler if everyone would just cooperate, David thought. What did he care if the Pharons or the Shard or anybody else got out of this place, so long as humanity did as well?

"You would care if they became your neighbors," said Navrel.

Raedawn looked at him, then at David. Harxae said, "Private thought," and she shrugged.

"So how long before we get there?" she asked.

"Most of one of your days," said Navrel.

A day to the center of the universe. David was amazed at the notion that all of the Maelstrom—hundreds of planets and thousands of asteroids—was now such a short distance across. Given the high acceleration the Kalirae ships were capable of, that meant it was maybe twice the width of the solar system at most. And his discovery might make it even shorter yet. When he was younger and more naive he might have considered such a situation to be a good thing, but after a lifetime of watching the nations of Earth squabble for resources and living space, he knew better. Bringing people closer together merely gave them more reasons to fight one another.

"You begin to understand," said Navrel.

Raedawn looked at David again with a peeved expression. "It's not polite to carry on half a conversation silently."

"I'm not trying to carry on a conversation," he said. "I'm just thinking."

"Well, think out loud. Or better yet, don't think at all. It was your thinking that got us into this mess in the first place."

How could he argue with that? If he hadn't decided to try to track down Earth and bring it home, he and Raedawn and Boris would still be happily squabbling over resources on Mars.

Navrel opened his mouth, but Raedawn said, "Not on your life," and he shut it again without speaking. She pulled the slowly drying front of her shirt away from her skin and said, "Look, if we're not in danger of dying right away, I'd like to clean up and get a little rest while I've got the chance. It's been a long day, and it looks like it's just going to get longer. Do you have a room with a shower and a bed in it anywhere on this ship?"

"You sleep in the rain?" asked Navrel.

"No. Jeez, you'd think someone who could read minds would—"

"Precisely," said Navrel. He and Harxae both smacked their lips in alien laughter.

She said nothing, just looked at them, and they immediately shut up. Harxae bowed his head and said, "Follow me." He led the way back to the doors at the rear of the control dome.

David tagged along, figuring he should at least learn where to find the bathroom, but when they got to her quarters, a palatial mansion of a suite that would put most luxury apartments to shame, Raedawn said, "Come on in. I could use somebody to wash my back."

"Oh. Sure."

She laughed. "You should see your expression."

He realized he was grinning like a goof, but he couldn't stop. "Why don't you at least show me where my room is first," he said to Harxae.

"You will require only one," said the alien.

"Are you—I mean—oh." He looked from Harxae to Raedawn, who was grinning now herself. "Okay."

"I will return for you when we reach the Tkona," said Harxae, stepping back into the corridor and letting the door slide shut.

"Don't let us get blown up in the meantime," David said, knowing the door wouldn't stop Harxae from picking up the thought.

Raedawn reached up and put her hands behind his neck. "Yeah, really," she said softly. "It would be a drag to get distracted at a time like this."

* * *

There wasn't even a scar. When they removed her blood-soaked clothing and washed the sticky brown residue from her skin, David and Raedawn could find no evidence that she had ever been shot. She didn't even feel any tenderness when David pressed on the spot; only ticklishness, which led to a long, loud game of "does *this* tickle?" in the shower, which led to a longer game of "so what does this feel like?" after they toweled off.

Later, as they rested somewhere near the middle of a bed that had to be extravagant even by Kalirae standards, David asked, "So what did it feel like to get shot?"

She was resting her head on his chest. She turned and bit him, not hard enough to draw blood, but enough to make him yelp in surprise and real pain. "No," she said, laying her head back down, "on second thought, I don't think it was like that at all. More like a bee sting. A really big bee, with a stinger as long as your finger."

"Ouch."

"That's what I thought. Then I fell down the stairs and I remember thinking very clearly, 'Shit, now I'm going to break something, too.' Then I tried to breathe and that didn't work so well, and I heard you shout 'No!' and I thought, 'This really isn't good.' I think that's when I realized I'd been shot."

Her voice had been growing louder and more animated, and he could feel her heartbeat picking up again. He said, "You don't have to talk about it if you don't want to."

"No, that's all right. I need to sort through it all, and I'd rather have someone to hold onto while I do it."

"Oh. Okay, then."

She laughed softly. "I remember being really embarrassed at the thought that you were going to land the ship in the hospital parking lot. I was all, 'Oh, jeez, he's going to get himself into even more trouble and it's all my fault.' "

"Like you got yourself shot on purpose."

"It's funny, but part of me figured I must have done something wrong, or it wouldn't have happened. I think that's the thing that surprised me the most. I've always thought I was a cynical bitch, but—"

"Me, too."

"Quiet, you, or I'll bite you again. As I was saying, I always thought I was cynical, but apparently some part of me down deep still thought that the universe was basically a fair place. Bad things wouldn't happen to people who didn't deserve them. Isn't that a laugh?"

"Hilarious."

"So I was lying there, bleeding and telling myself what a horrible person I must be, and you were flying me maybe three blocks to the hospital, and I see all these little mushrooms rolling around on the deck. I thought I was hallucinating, you know? But then I heard them rattling, and one of them bounced over close enough that I could see it, and I realized they were bullets."

David remembered the ricochets smacking into the back wall until he closed the airlock. Space Force weapons used soft bullets so they wouldn't penetrate the hull if they were fired on board a ship, but they made a nastier wound.

"I remember looking at that lump of metal on the deck and thinking, 'One of those things is inside me.' It just felt so weird." She rolled sideways and pressed her fingers against the skin beneath her right breast. "You know what feels weird now?"

"No, what?"

"*Not* being shot so quickly afterward. I barely had time to get used to the idea that I had been, but you know, it's happened to a lot of people and I was thinking, 'Well, I guess this is the way it works.' But then all of a sudden it wasn't anymore, and I had to start thinking about what all *that* meant."

He took the opportunity to kiss where her fingers had touched. "What does it mean?"

"What's the meaning of life? I have no more idea than I ever did, but look at it this way. In a couple more hours we're going to do something even crazier than what we did when we left Mars. Half the population of this nightmare place apparently wants us dead, and I half expect they'll get their wish. So this is where I choose to spend my last hours. What does that tell you?"

"A lot," he said. He looked into her green eyes, brushed a lock of her dark hair away from her forehead. "I love you, too."

"Don't sound so surprised," she said, tickling him playfully.

"Well, I *am* surprised. I used to think you were . . ."

"A cynical bitch."

"Right. But then everything started happening at once, and I sort of forgot about that, and, well, here we are."

"Here we are," she said, laying her head back on his chest.

They were up and dressed again by the time Harxae came for them. Raedawn's clothes had taken a good deal of scrubbing to get the dried blood out, but fortunately the clothing was all black. Drying it off had proved the hardest part until they discovered that the bathroom could be turned into a sauna, whereupon they cranked up the heat and toasted it dry in a matter of minutes.

David was glad of the heat as well. Seeing all that red-tinged water swirling down the drain had made him shiver. *How fragile we are*, he thought. How fragile, yet humanity had learned to harness such immense amounts of energy. They had built weapons that could completely vaporize a person. Their spaceships—hell, even their hovercars—channeled forces strong enough that an accident was often fatal. A simple power cord could kill if its insulation was compromised. People faced death from all directions every day and hardly thought about it, yet their lives depended upon everything working smoothly. They had grown complacent.

He wondered if that was such a bad thing. Maybe that was the ultimate triumph of civilization: to make traumatic death so rare that people became complacent.

That was about to change. The Union and the Neo-Soviets had been teetering on the brink of Armageddon for years, neither side truly understanding what they were about to unleash, and now Earth had been plunged into even greater chaos. People were about to learn just how fragile their world and their lives actually were.

Maybe, like Raedawn, if they survived it, they would gain a new appreciation for what really mattered.

27

The Tkona was much closer now. When they stepped out into the control room, they saw its bright blue-white glow spread across half the heavens. The clear dome had darkened to near opaqueness to prevent its light from blinding the crew, but David could still sense its intense energy in the way it washed color from everything and increased the contrast to stark white or inky night.

The ship was passing over the innermost ring of worlds. There were few actual planets left intact; collisions had split their crusts and spewed their molten cores into space, where the magma had cooled to form asteroids that had in turn smashed themselves to rubble. Electrical discharges thousands of kilometers long arced between them, evidence of the enormous magnetic field that reached out from the spinning core.

It looked like the accretion disk of a black hole must look. David wondered what the radiation level was inside the ship, but he didn't have any familiar instruments to check, and there wasn't much he could do about it if it was lethal anyway.

He looked behind them. Four points of light moved

against the churning background, apparently all of their pursuers who cared to venture this close to chaos. To the sides and above, the other three Kalirae ships held formation.

"Even odds now, eh?" he asked Harxae.

"Those are Shard," said the alien.

"Meaning . . . ?"

"Meaning the odds are nowhere near even."

Raedawn said, "Who are these Shard guys, anyway? You talk about them like they eat bogeymen for lunch."

"Pharons eat bogeymen for lunch," Harxae said. "The Shard don't eat, but if they did, they would eat Pharons for lunch."

"Oh."

"Perhaps I exaggerate, but not by much. They were once energy beings. When their world was drawn into the Maelstrom, the Tkona disrupted their energy matrices, and they were forced to take on physical form. They chose a crystalline structure." He shook his head. "You are thinking of hard, brittle crystals. No. Think nanites. They can shift their form more easily than you or I. They can flow like water when need be. They can form weapons from their own substance and power them with energy from their very essence. And they hate their imprisonment in physical form even worse than we hate our imprisonment in the Maelstrom."

"Infinite power in a perpetual bad mood, eh?" Raedawn asked.

"You begin to grasp the problem."

David said, "How many are there on each of those ships?"

"Each ship carries one being. The Shard intelligence spreads throughout the vessel, so you could think of them as the ship itself, but the vital spark is protected in the core."

Nano-malleable, powerful, and well shielded. David began to grasp the problem as well.

Navrel was on the other side of the dome, talking with four other Kalirae. Harxae led the humans over to them, and Navrel said, "We have reconfigured some of our weapons to provide magnetic pulses. I gathered the necessary information from your mind as you rested. I hope you are not offended."

David had sensed nothing. Now he felt more embarrassed than offended, but he supposed he had no reason to feel either. Mind reading was like breathing to these people; they had no concept of privacy.

"Where do you plan to use these pulse bombs?" he asked.

Navrel pointed at the inner edge of the ring system. "See those tendrils of dark matter?"

Even with the dome filtering most of the light, David had to squint into the glare, but he saw what Navrel was talking about. Long, snakelike tentacles of blackness writhed back and forth, lashing out at the leading edge of the ring. Where they hit matter, flares erupted, and huge chunks of rock were ripped loose. They looked very much like the tendrils that had reached for Earth when the dark cloud had first appeared in space around it.

"I don't think we really want to go in there," he said. "Have you tried setting off a pulse out here?"

"For what reason? The anomalous space is there."

"You should have dug a little deeper while you were in my head. One of the things I discovered back on Mars is that you don't have to be right on top of the anomaly in order to punch through. As long as space is stressed enough, you can make a new hole nearby. By the looks of that, I'd say it's plenty stressed right where we are."

Navrel looked out at the burning white hole in space. "We have many pulse bombs. Let us try it."

He had hardly spoken before missile fire streaked from the front of the ship. It rushed out in front of them until it was just a speck against the huge backdrop of stellar fire, then detonated in a tiny burst of extra light.

The effect was instantaneous. Tendrils from the core lashed out toward the explosion, but another black splotch appeared in space around it, swallowing up the light like an ink stain spreading on paper.

A malevolent, whirling ink stain that spit lightning like a short circuit in a power station. It was far more energetic than the cloud that had brought their shuttle through from the solar system, far more energetic even than the one that had swallowed Earth. And somehow it felt far, far more menacing as well.

"Get ready to blow it open just before we get there," David said. "This looks like the entrance side rather than the exit, and I don't think we want to go in there blind."

"Agreed."

The ship drew closer, and the dark cloud reached out to meet it, but before it could make contact, another missile streaked out toward it and disappeared into the darkness. A moment later it flashed with light and billowed outward, great bright fissures opening in its surface as the flood of extra energy overwhelmed its ability to hold itself together.

David could see nothing inside it. If there were stars, the intense light from the Tkona and the explosion itself blotted them out.

"Do you see anything?" he asked.

Navrel took a moment to answer, probably polling everyone in the control dome first. "No. But the quality of light is different from the Tkona. Wherever it leads, it is somewhere other than here."

It wasn't collapsing again like the others had done. In fact, darkness reappeared at the outer edges as it continued to expand. "Let's send a probe through first," said David.

"We don't have that luxury." Navrel pointed back toward the Shard ships, which had fired a barrage of missiles at them. At least that's what they looked like at first, but as they drew closer David realized they were zigzagging back and forth like lightning bolts.

"Plasma conduits," Navrel said. "We cannot intercept them." He turned to the anomaly again, and even though he said nothing aloud, all four Kalirae ships accelerated hard into it.

David and Raedawn grabbed one another and braced themselves for impact. The Kalirae apparently trusted their gravity generators; none of them even hung on to a console for support, but they should have. The ship shuddered and groaned as grainy gray darkness enveloped it. David and Raedawn did an impromptu little dance as first one of them lost their balance and nearly fell, then the other. They heard muffled thuds and curses through the fog, then the ship burst out into free space again.

The Tkona was gone. Either that or they were inside it, but wherever they were, it wasn't a good place to be. The entire sky burned fiercely bright, and the other Kalirae ships looked twisted, as if seen through a fishbowl.

David tapped his watch into calculator mode and called up the value of pi: 0.167.

"Get us out of here!" he ordered. "Go back through, now!"

Just then, a plasma bolt hit the ship to their right. It lurched forward with the impact, lightning crackling up and down its flanks, then the entire ship erupted in a fiery explosion. The Kalirae on their ship all jerked as if they had been hit as well. They probably had, David supposed. At the moment he was glad he wasn't telepathic. He was ashamed to realize that he also was glad it wasn't a ship full of humans that had died.

The debris from the explosion flew outward, but instead of traveling in a straight line, it looped around in tight spirals.

"What the hell?" Raedawn asked.

He said, "Space is so curved here that a straight line is the *longest* distance between two points." If he needed proof that Lamott was right, this was certainly compelling evidence. The normal universe didn't have areas where pi was a variable; this must be another part of the Maelstrom.

Their ship and the remaining two whirled around to face the anomaly just as two of the four Shard vessels hove into view. Everyone fired at once, and space filled with swirling missiles and jagged plasma bolts, but there was no way to aim. It was like a fire in a rocket factory; there was nothing to do but duck and hope you didn't get hit.

"Head into the anomaly!" David said. "We've got to blow it open again and get out of here."

The Kalirae ship edged forward, but the anomaly veered away. The pilots tried to correct, but each time they did, their target dodged again as if it were a living thing trying to avoid them.

"What the hell, try a spiral," David said.

Two missiles roared past just over the dome. One scored a lucky hit on a Shard ship and blasted a third of it loose, but the rest of it pulled together to fill the gap and continued firing plasma bolts.

A second Kalirae ship took a hit that blew off one of its

back fins. Debris roared out into space from the hull breach, and the ship spiraled around, still under thrust, until it plunged into the anomaly and disappeared from sight.

"That's the hard way," Raedawn said, "but it looks like it worked."

The Shard seemed to be having just as much trouble navigating. They swerved this way and that, still firing plasma bolts, but the one that had already been hit once accidentally zapped the other. It crackled with electrical discharge and exploded just like the first Kalirae ship.

David whipped his head back and forth, trying to watch everything at once. The Kalirae all gazed out in different directions, unmoving, and no doubt seeing better than him. They continued to run for the anomaly, which was visible only as a bright turbulent vortex in the general brightness, but suddenly the second Shard vessel loomed directly ahead. The Kalirae immediately fired more missiles, and this time the range was close enough that at least half hit their target. The explosions ripped it into three chunks that spiraled away, still crackling with lightning. One drifted into the anomaly, and the second Kalirae ship followed it in.

That left only the Kalirae flagship. Navrel's crew guided it closer and closer, slowing down and nudging it this way and that toward the end, until the grainy darkness once more enveloped them.

"Are you still in contact with the other ships?" David asked.

"Barely," said Navrel.

"Everybody has to fire at once. High explosives at short range. It's not enough just to open the gateway; you've got to bust it apart, or it'll just close up and drop us back into this part of the Maelstrom again."

"Understood."

David felt completely exposed here in the wide expanse of the Kalirae control room. The thought of two other ships out there firing blind into the fog made his skin crawl. He pulled Raedawn close to him and held her tight while he waited for death to rain down out of the void.

There was no countdown. He didn't even hear the order to fire. The gray fog merely erupted into light too bright for even the opaqued dome to deflect, and a moment later the three Kalirae ships were back at the edge of the Tkona.

Where the other two Shard were waiting for them.

28

They didn't fire. David wondered why, then he saw the fragment of the Shard ship that had come back through the gateway with them. It was right off the bow of their ship, and it wasn't dead yet. Apparently the Shard cared enough about their own to hold their fire, or maybe they wanted to find out what it had seen before resuming hostilities that would surely doom it.

The Kalirae didn't wait to see how long that would last. They poured everything they had at the two intact Shard, plus a few extra shots for the fragment. Then, even as their missiles streaked outward, the ships all split apart and headed for the Tkona.

At least that's what David thought they were doing, but the one that had already been hit rushed straight toward one of the Shard vessels. It fired such a barrage of missiles that it looked like it had drive flame coming out both ends. The Shard ship tried to intercept all the incoming warheads, but it was completely overwhelmed. It tried to evade the ones that got through, but one scored a direct hit and two more ripped pieces off the edges. That didn't kill the ship; it had enough life left to fire on the Kalirae ship point-blank, engulfing it in plasma.

It was too late. The Kalirae struck the Shard before it blew, and the explosion took out both ships.

The fragment had become gravel. That left just one intact Shard and two Kalirae, but the Shard surged after them and the Kalirae didn't seem inclined to turn and fight. They aimed for the center of the vortex instead.

"You're not going deeper in there?" David said.

Navrel didn't answer.

"We have little choice," Harxae said. "There are more Shard on the way."

David looked behind and saw a dozen or more specks of light moving steadily closer. Harxae pointed off to the side, and then to the other side, where there were even more.

"I think maybe it's time you called in reinforcements," Raedawn said.

Harxae looked away. "I didn't wish to worry you before now, but we have been unable to contact the homeworld since we approached the Tkona."

"So we're completely on our own."

"Yes."

"Great."

David eyed the ships approaching from the side. "We'll never make it to the actual vortex before they intercept us," he said.

"That is true," said Harxae. "I'm afraid we'll have to make another gateway of our own."

"Not if it leads us back there," David said.

Harxae held out his arms. "I think I know what happened before. Remember, I can feel the curvature of space. We were in a very tight region at the moment we fired our magnetic pulse bomb. If we choose a flatter area of space this time, perhaps the results will be different."

"Maybe. It might just drop us right into the middle of *that*." David pointed at the Tkona.

"Do we have a choice? Space is entirely too empty here. We have nowhere to hide, and nowhere to run. It is time to leap from the train, off the bridge, and into the river of chance."

David looked at the oncoming ships again. He counted twenty-three of them. Even jumping off the bridge didn't seem like much of a strategy, but he couldn't think of anything better.

"All right," he said finally. "Let's do it."

Harxae backed away and spread his arms wide, then turned slowly around. The two Kalirae ships veered off to the left in tight formation, then banked upward as he directed them toward flatter space. David checked pi on his watch: 3.167. As close to normal as they were likely to get.

Harxae was apparently satisfied with it, too. The Kalirae ships were firing a steady curtain of fire behind them to keep the Shard at bay; now they fired a single missile forward. It drew ahead a few kilometers, then exploded, and another dark cloud blossomed out in its magnetic wake.

Both ships arrowed straight into it. This time everyone braced for the impact, but the effects were much less severe than before. It's the boundary effect between different curvatures, David thought. Less boundary means less effect.

As soon as they burst out into free space, both ships immediately spun around and braked to a stop just outside the gateway. David watched for the Shard ship to come through, but Raedawn's gasp of surprise brought his attention to her face, then upward to whatever she was looking at with such an expression of wonder.

They were near a planet. It looked Earth-like, with blue oceans and brown land and streaks of white cloud in its atmosphere. It looked impossibly serene for its location: the Tkona was a bright whorl completely surrounding it. It was inside the swirling chaos, and though lightning bolts and tendrils of dark matter lashed out all around it, none touched it.

"It's beautiful," Raedawn said.

"It's fragile as glass." David turned to Harxae. "What's keeping the Tkona at bay?"

Navrel hadn't spoken since the other Kalirae ships were destroyed. Now he turned to David and said, "I don't know. We have observed pockets of stability in the Inner Ring, but none so deep as this."

"Is anyone alive here?" Raedawn asked.

"We detect no sign of it," Navrel said, "but there is so much interfer—"

The Shard ship burst through the anomaly, already firing its plasma bolts at random. The Kalirae ships immediately fired back, and for a moment all three poured enough energy at one another to rival the sun in brightness. Then the other Kalirae ship took a direct hit, and lightning bolts crackled up and down its length. The crew must have known they were dead, but they did the one last thing they could do: they fired their engines and rammed the Shard at full acceleration, driving both ships back into the anomaly.

Just before they disappeared, the Kalirae ship exploded. The blast rippled through the white cloud, but didn't tear it apart. It had happened a few seconds too soon.

"Fire!" David said. "Fire straight into it!"

Navrel looked at him, then back at the anomaly, but no missiles flew from their ship.

"There are two dozen more Shard about to come through that gateway," David said.

"But nobody on the other side knows what we just learned. No radio or telepathic signal can penetrate the Tkona. We must go back and tell them."

"We wouldn't survive thirty seconds on the other side. Maybe we can open another gateway after we close this one, but I'm not convinced that's the best thing to do anyway. Do we really want this ability to open gateways from place to place to become common knowledge in the Maelstrom?"

Navrel looked over at Harxae. All across the great domed control room, the Kalirae crew froze in deep thought.

Then they slowly began to move again. Navrel looked back to David and said, "You shame us. Once, before we were cast into the Maelstrom, we were capable of such altruism. Pray that your race continues to produce people who can act as you do."

Missiles flashed away from their ships into the churning white cloud. A few roared on through, trailing streamers of other space behind them, but there was still a Shard ship somewhere inside there, and at least a few missiles hit it. There were half a dozen flashes, then a spectacular fireball that tore the anomaly apart, revealing the naked gateway for just a second before it collapsed.

That second was enough. From their vantage point they could see the outer edge of the Tkona thrashing its angry tentacles out into the chaotic inner ring of debris, and closer at hand the Shard ships bearing down on the gateway, their weapons already firing.

Then it closed off forever, slicing off the war like a guillotine taking off the head of the last revolutionary.

A single burst of plasma made it through the opening. It was a partial shot at that; the rear half of the bolt had been left on the other side. David had seen so many of them in the past few minutes that he watched it with cool detachment, waiting for it to flash harmlessly past. But it came straight on, and he had just enough time to realize they were in trouble before it hit.

The ship lurched backward. A moment later the gravity failed, casting everyone up into the dome. Most of the crew members grabbed something and hauled themselves back down, but David and Raedawn had been holding on to each other and by the time they reached out for support they were already a few meters off the deck and rising.

Harxae reached upward and snagged David's leg, drawing them back down. He turned to Navrel, and the two locked eyes in silent communication again.

"We must get you to safety," Navrel finally said to David. "You are the hope of escape for my race and others." He said to Harxae, "You know what to do. Get him to safety. He is the important one."

"Oh, thanks a lot," said Raedawn.

Overhead, the surface of the dome crackled with energy. David steeled himself for the explosion he knew was coming. The other ships had lasted only a few seconds before the plasma charge had overloaded their power plants. This hadn't been a complete burst, but it looked bad enough to do the job.

Then Harxae whirled around, grabbed David and Raedawn in his powerful arms, and leaped toward the doors. He bounced off the door frame, careened into the corridor beyond, and pulled himself up short at the first doorway beyond it. It was open, and the interior was the first small room they had seen on the ship. It held two wide benches with shoulder straps for maybe ten occupants to sit side by side and a single bucket seat at the far end facing a small circular window.

"Lifeboat?" David asked wonderingly.

Harxae shoved them down on the right-hand bench, then pulled himself inside and slapped the control that closed the door. "Hang on," he said as he took command of the ship and pressed one of the control buttons.

There was a loud bang, and the lifeboat lurched under heavy acceleration. David and Raedawn clutched at the straps, but they wound up plastered against the door, afraid to move for fear of hitting the wrong button and pitching themselves out into space.

Then came a clatter like hail on a metal roof just behind them, and the lifeboat shook violently.

"That was the ship blowing up, wasn't it?" asked Raedawn.

Harxae didn't answer, but the debris flashing past the window was all the answer they needed.

"I'm sorry," said David. He felt stupid saying it. The words were never enough, but they were all he had to give.

Harxae steadied the ship, then lowered their acceleration to a quarter gee or so. David and Raedawn crawled uphill to the end of the benches nearest his chair and strapped themselves in across from each other where they could both see out the window.

The new planet glistened below them. Harxae's fingers ran over the controls, and undecipherable strings of alien figures appeared on a monitor set in the middle of the control panel. "How hot do you like it?" he asked.

"What?" David was too stunned to make sense of the question. He'd just watched everything he knew vanish for the second time. His home was now two universes away, and Harxae was asking about the temperature?

"Living conditions," Harxae said. "What environmental extremes do you prefer?"

"Living conditions? What?"

"This is not a shuttle. It's a life pod. We get one landing, and I detect no sign of technological civilization below, so we had best make a good choice the first time." He looked back at them and said, "I am not fond of what you call snow."

"Me either," said Raedawn.

"Wait a minute." David took a deep breath, trying to clear his head. "You're talking about picking a place to settle down? As in live out the rest of our lives?"

"Is he always this slow?" asked Harxae.

That had to be a thought robbed from Raedawn's subconscious. He ignored it. "We're not even going to try to go back?"

"You may try if you wish," said Harxae, "but we have no spaceship and no pulse bombs. Perhaps your descendants will be able to create them."

"Descendants." He glanced across at Raedawn, who looked just as stunned as he. "We're supposed to play Adam and Eve?"

Harxae snorted. "Whether it is play or not will depend to a great degree upon where we land. How warm do you like it? How much vegetation? Do you prefer mountains, or plains? Your minds are not clear on any of these subjects."

"We're . . . not used to thinking in those terms," Raedawn said. Her eyes were still on David's, and he almost laughed when he realized he'd instinctively sat up a little straighter and squared his shoulders.

"You will grow accustomed to it," said Harxae.

David supposed they would. It was either that or die, and the human survival instinct was strong enough to change practically anyone's behavior when their life depended on it. And the lives of their family.

Assuming they could actually have one. "Even if the Tkona doesn't fry us first, inbreeding would turn our progeny into lobsters within a few generations."

Harxae said, "I have healing powers. I am not as fast as a trained medic, but over time I can stabilize your genetic code."

"What about you?" Raedawn said. "You're going to just grow old and die here while we restart humanity?"

"I certainly hope not," said Harxae. "I still have a good two hundred years left. Plenty of time to start a family of my own."

"But—there's only one of you."

Harxae made his lip-smacking laugh. "You are thinking in human terms. Your way may be more entertaining, but mine is more efficient. I will restart the Kalirae race here myself."

More likely they would die side by side at the whim of the Tkona, but the planet certainly looked untroubled by its chaotic surroundings. It had survived this long; who knew how much longer it could last. Maybe long enough for two races to grow up side by side from the very beginning.

Even if that was possible, could they actually live together, or would they descend into warfare like the other races thrust together in the Maelstrom?

David studied the new world below them. It was a big planet. There should be room enough for everyone for a very long time.

He couldn't deny the lure of the challenge. He'd always considered himself a pioneer, and this looked like a wonderful place to try it. He'd never really felt at home anywhere and had yearned for one somewhere deep down. But at what price would he get one now? They'd been cast away from everyone and everything they knew without even the chance to say good-bye.

He thought of Boris, lying in his hospital bed while the regenerator repaired his broken bones. A nurse would come in to check his progress, he would ask what had happened to his friends, and the nurse would tell him that they had died in battle. He would lie back, saddened by the news, and maybe later when he had healed he would drink a toast to their memory, but then he would go on. He had his own unknown fate to live.

Uncertainty seemed to be the hallmark of the Maelstrom. But it looked like David actually had a choice, at least for the moment. He looked out at the new planet and said, "Mountains. Someplace with a fishing stream."

"Wait a minute," said Raedawn. "I want ocean. Sandy beaches, coconut palms, grass huts. You know. Tropical paradise."

"With mountains," David said.

Harxae turned around in his chair. "I prefer desert."

"Why am I not surprised?"

They looked at one another, three refugees from another dimension with their lives quite literally laid out before them. This was the moment when they would decide how the future would go. Could they agree on this most fundamental question?

Raedawn laughed softly. "It sounds like we want southern California."

California. David had never considered living there, not with its overpopulation and pollution and acres of pavement. But someplace *like* that, before civilization had overrun it . . . yes, that could work. And maybe they would have the chance to do it right this time.

Harxae nodded. "There is no California here, but I understand the concept." He turned back to the controls.

David reached across the narrow space between himself and Raedawn. She smiled her enigmatic "don't count on it" smile, but she reached out to meet him halfway as the lifeboat kissed the top of the atmosphere.

VISIT WARNER ASPECT ONLINE!

THE WARNER ASPECT HOMEPAGE
You'll find us at: www.twbookmark.com then by clicking on Science Fiction and Fantasy.

NEW AND UPCOMING TITLES
Each month we feature our new titles and reader favorites.

AUTHOR INFO
Author bios, bibliographies and links to personal websites.

CONTESTS AND OTHER FUN STUFF
Advance galley giveaways, autographed copies, and more.

THE ASPECT BUZZ
What's new, hot and upcoming from Warner Aspect: awards news, best-sellers, movie tie-in information . . .